There had to be

The Mac Edwards Ra... [obscured] ...great father. He woul... [obscured] ...child. He would have kept her safe from harm. He wouldn't have become the man portrayed in the Child Services case file before her.

With shaking hands that betrayed her lack of emotional detachment, Rachel dived deeper into the case file.

Amanda is an angry young girl, and it is my opinion that there is probably some underlying abuse between Mr. Edwards and his daughter. In light of this and Amanda's growing criminal record, she needs to be removed from the home.

Rachel had to read the words five times before they sank in. There was no way her former best friend could be abusing his daughter!

Rachel knew she should not take this case. It was a conflict of interest if there ever was one. What she *should* have done was march up to her boss and say, "I know this guy. Loved him, actually. I definitely broke his heart. So I shouldn't be their social worker."

She should have done that.

But she didn't.

Dear Reader,

I am so thrilled about my Harlequin Superromance debut, *Family at Stake!* Superromance novels started my love affair with romance, so I am tickled to be a part of such an enduring facet of romance fiction. I actually had a box of Harlequin Superromance novels under my bed at a very early age (I am sure most of you did, too). And many of those books–having been packed up and moved dozens of times over the years–are still on my keeper shelf at home. The things we do for good books!

With *Family at Stake* I tried my own twist on some of my favorite romantic themes–reunited lovers, at-risk children, single fathers, betrayal and, of course, forgiveness. Mac is easily my favorite hero to date–I love a man who struggles to keep his world together even as it unravels around him. And cracking Rachel's icy protective shell was one of the most challenging conflicts I've tried to solve. Even as I tried to change her–or compromise with her character–she wouldn't let me.

I hope you enjoy my take on Harlequin Superromance books. Please feel free to drop me a line and tell me what you think at www.molly-okeefe.com.

Happy reading!

Molly O'Keefe

FAMILY AT STAKE
Molly O'Keefe

TORONTO • NEW YORK • LONDON
AMSTERDAM • PARIS • SYDNEY • HAMBURG
STOCKHOLM • ATHENS • TOKYO • MILAN • MADRID
PRAGUE • WARSAW • BUDAPEST • AUCKLAND

ISBN-13: 978-0-373-71365-3
ISBN-10:   0-373-71365-7

FAMILY AT STAKE

Copyright © 2006 by Molly Fader.

www.eHarlequin.com

Printed in U.S.A.

ABOUT THE AUTHOR

Molly O'Keefe grew up in a small town outside Chicago. How she ended up in Toronto, Canada, she's not quite sure. She sold her first romance to Harlequin at age twenty-five and hasn't looked back! She lives in Toronto with her husband, son, cat and the largest heap of dirty laundry in North America.

For Mick and his Old Man—I love you.

PROLOGUE

May 20, 1992

"GOODBYE, NEW SPRINGS!" Rachel Filmore ripped off her purple nylon graduation gown and tossed it up in the air. It unfurled in the breeze and drifted into the rock quarry like a shadow against the twilight sky.

"Goodbye, Mom!" She ripped off the cap, ignoring the pull of the bobby pins that tore at her curly hair and flung that into the air, too.

"And last but not least, goodbye, Dad, may you rot in hell." She dug her fake high school diploma—which said her real diploma would be mailed to her—out of her backpack and sent it sailing into the abyss at her feet.

It had been handed to her a few hours ago at the graduation ceremony.

"Your name is on that," Rachel's best friend, Mac Edwards, pointed out with a laugh. "Someone might find it."

"Like anyone is going to care." She looked over the edge, but in the darkness she couldn't see the bottom of the quarry, much less her graduation gown spread out among the rocks. "Maybe they'll think I jumped," she muttered, feeling the gravitational pull of all that space between her and the bottom. Sometimes when she stood really still on the ledge like this it seemed like the ground reached up for her.

"They'll think I jumped just to get out of this dumb town. I swear, Mac. New Springs is like a noose around our necks."

"That's not funny," Mac murmured, and Rachel turned to face him. He sat on the hard-packed earth, his own graduation gown in a heap beside him. He still wore the cap, though. He had tilted it at what he called a "rakish angle." He was always trying to be like Humphrey Bogart or some other old actor. Mac said they had class. Rachel didn't know one way or another; she never stayed awake during those boring old movies.

But Mac looked cute with his hat like that.

Something weird was going on with Mac these days. Weirder than normal. His face was changing. He suddenly had cheekbones and a jawline and his eyes…well. Rachel found herself unable to look too long into those eyes.

He seemed older, like a man.

His body had changed last year. Almost overnight, it'd gotten bigger. Where he'd been skinny he'd developed muscle. He must have grown five inches in the span of two months.

The coaches had tried to get him to go out for the football and basketball teams. He didn't do it, but she knew he was flattered that they'd asked. She *also* knew that Margaret McCormick had been coming to his locker between classes, tossing her hair around and bending over to pick things up from the floor in front of him. Rachel had caught him looking at Margaret's butt.

Margaret had joined the Science Club and had even asked him to tutor her, since everyone knew that he was a science genius. He'd helped Margaret one night, but Mac wouldn't tell Rachel what had happened. He said they'd just studied, but he'd blushed when he said it.

Maybe that was what was weird, Rachel thought as she studied her friend. *Mac is a little mysterious.*

Her belly did that long slow roll it'd been doing whenever Mac was around. That was weird, too. She had known Mac since freshman year and now she was hot for her best friend. Seriously hot—as in "let's make out and get naked" hot. She didn't know what to do about it, except of course ignore it, which she had been trying for a few months now, and that just made her more crazy.

She wanted to do whatever he and Margaret had done.

But she didn't know how to get from best friend to naked all in one night. And one night was all they had left.

"You gonna toss your gown in, too?" she asked, sitting next to him. She flipped her skirt up over her knees and thought about grabbing her sweatshirt from the bag, but it was still hot out and the tank top she wore was fine.

"Nah." He reclined against the smooth, round rock at their backs. "Thought I'd burn it. Someone said you can get high off the fumes."

She chuckled and leaned back with him. She brushed his shoulder with hers—totally on purpose—and her breath caught at the zing that raced along her skin.

Touch me. Touch me. Touch me.

If she opened her mouth, she was sure those words would come pouring out like sand.

"Look what your brother gave me today" Mac dug into his own bag and pulled out a small piece of wood.

Her vision blurred with hot tears.

She wished she could pretend there was no Jesse, no little brother she was being forced to leave behind. Maybe then it wouldn't feel as if she was drowning all the time.

She picked up the piece of avocado wood that Jesse had whittled into a four-inch-high tree with branches and roots using his twenty-year-old Swiss Army knife.

She ran her thumb along the ridges and the veins in the leaves and felt her heart breaking.

"It's amazing," Mac whispered. "I mean, the kid is eleven. What eleven-year-old can do that?"

Rachel shrugged and handed it back to him. "He's something," she whispered.

"Rachel—" Mac's tone was soft and sympathetic, and the hand that cupped her shoulder burned her to the bone. An ugly mix of emotions inside of her—a seething, poisonous combination—tried to leak out. *Don't ruin this night. It's my last night. Don't cry. Don't, Rachel.* She pressed down all the impotent anger and raging sadness and turned a bright smile to her old friend.

"Hey, I brought something." She remembered what she had pilfered from the back of the fridge. Since she was leaving tomorrow she didn't need to worry about her father finding out and losing his mind. She rummaged in her backpack. "It's probably warm by now," she muttered, and pulled out the bottle of champagne she'd wrapped in towels to keep cool. "Ta-da!"

"Wow, champagne," Mac nodded. "Awesome. Since we're not having graduation parties—"

"Who needs crappy cake when you can have lukewarm champagne, huh?" she asked. She knew just how sad this was, which was why they had to joke about it. All of their classmates were having parties with volleyball nets set up in the backyard and coolers of pop and beer. But Rachel's and Mac's parents just couldn't get it together to put a special dinner on the table to celebrate their kids' achievements.

"Mom always says it's supposed to be for a special occasion, but the dumb bottle's been sitting in the back of the fridge forever." *There's no such thing as a special occasion at my house,* she thought, and fumbled with the top of the bottle. "How am I supposed to open this dumb thing?"

"Let me have that," Mac said, and tore off the foil. He stuck his thumbs under the cork, and his arm, pressed against hers, flexed, the veins that had suddenly appeared in his forearms strained against his skin. Rachel swallowed hard, swamped with new painful feelings.

"How do you know how to do this?" she asked. Maybe he and Margaret had champagne.

"Cary Grant," he muttered, preoccupied with the bottle.

The cork popped and the spray shot all over their feet. Rachel screamed and jerked her sandals out of the way. Mac took a giant swig, catching most of the foam.

"Perfect," he said, and wiped his mouth. His eyes were sparkly and filled with fun and they made her drunk enough. She didn't need champagne. He handed her the bottle and Rachel took it, all too aware that she was pressing the glass that had been on his mouth against her lips.

The champagne fizzed, sweet and cool down her throat. It *was* perfect.

"So?" He bent his knees and slung his long arms around them. He looked up at the stars and she knew he was searching out the Big Dipper and Cassiopeia.

He always looked for those first. *Gotta get my bearings,* he'd say.

Rachel took another gulp of the fizzy booze.

"Tomorrow, huh?"

"Yeah." She handed him the bottle.

"I can still give you a ride. San Luis Obispo isn't that far."

"Right, like The Jerk is going to give you the car."

"Screw him," he muttered, kicking at a rock that shot off the ledge. Rachel heard it clatter to the bottom. He took a long pull from the champagne bottle. She filled her lungs with as much air as possible and promised this would be the last time she tried.

"Come with me," she said in a rush.

"Rach—"

"You've got awesome grades—"

"And zero money." He rolled his head against the rock. "We've talked about this like a dozen times."

"I'm going early so I can get a job. You can get a job, too. We can bag groceries, or work with a landscaper. You'd like that. Working with the..." She trailed off. She knew begging wasn't doing any good. She had gotten the scholarship and he hadn't even applied. Even bagging groceries wouldn't make enough to cover books.

And Mac wasn't going to leave his mom, not while she was married to The Jerk.

Rachel nodded and took another swig of the champagne before handing it back to him. *What am*

I going to do without you? she thought, staring up at the sky. The world suddenly loomed too large without Mac beside her. All the spaces inside of her that she thought would be filled with excitement and hope and joy about college were vacant. Empty. All she felt was an anguished longing for her best friend and a sickening wish that things were different.

"It would be stupid to ask you to stay, huh?" he whispered, and her eyes flew to his in surprise. "I mean you—"

"I can't, Mac," she breathed, wondering what brought this on. "He kicked me out. He said after I graduated he—"

"He didn't want to see you," Mac finished, nodding. "I know." He drank some more from the bottle. She watched the shifting muscles in his throat as he swallowed. They were about three-quarters through the champagne and he'd had most of it.

Must be why he's saying such crazy things, she thought. *Stay? What would I do?*

"We can get married," he said, and, for a moment, Rachel thought she was dreaming. "That way you could stay." He looked at her, his blond hair gleaming white in the moonlight. His face was so handsome to her, so full and real and tight with a want that her body answered.

Heady, reckless desire bloomed in her.

"Married?" she breathed, unsure of what she thought or felt past the solid thumping of her heart.

Mac put down the bottle and turned toward her, and Rachel was caught by the expression on his face. That was why she couldn't stand to meet his eyes these days, because everything he felt about her was right there.

"I…ah…I love you." He swallowed hard. "I mean, you are my best—"

Rachel didn't know why she did it. To stop him from saying such things, or to stop herself from answering with promises that she might not be able to keep. She didn't know but she leaned forward and pressed her mouth to his.

She closed her eyes tight and listened to him gasp.

Please, please, please. She didn't know what she was asking for, but there was some nameless ache in her that had to be met. *I need you. I've always needed you. What will I do without you?*

"Rachel, what are you going to do?" He pulled away from her and the cold air between them felt like a knife against her skin. "I can't do this if you're just going to leave…."

"I'll stay," she lied, knowing she couldn't, but she couldn't let him walk away from her right now.

"Rach—" His smile was beautiful and it killed her. She kissed him and closed her eyes.

His tongue touched her closed mouth and his arms came around her, brushing the bare skin of her arms and her shoulders. His fingers found the sensitive nape of her neck and she moaned.

Mac's tongue licked slowly into her mouth as they carefully leaned back on the ground.

She was seventeen and Mac was going to be the first boy she ever had sex with. Tonight. Her shirt came off and his hand cupped her breast, and that was a first, too. He peeled off his T-shirt. He was lean and beautiful and her fingers touched him, traced the muscles of his chest, his stomach. It was all new.

This didn't change what would happen tomorrow. But tonight, in the moonlight, held tightly against Mac's body, she was able to pretend it didn't matter.

CHAPTER ONE

Present day

OH, BOY, RACHEL FILMORE thought as she paused in the doorway and watched her friend Olivia Hernandez work herself right into a mental health crisis, *it's like watching a train wreck.*

"Hello?" She knocked on the door as quietly as she could, but Olivia still jumped out of her seat.

"Stop doing that," Olivia breathed, clutching the ruffled neck of her pink T-shirt.

"It's knocking, sweetheart, and it's polite." Rachel smiled and leaned against the door frame of her boss's office.

"Give me five more minutes," Olivia said, then swiveled toward her computer screen.

"You said that twenty minutes ago," Rachel reminded her.

"I know, I know, but I'm right in the middle—"

"Code red," Rachel interrupted, and Olivia's head snapped up.

"Realmente?" Olivia looked around at the tow-

ering stacks of files as if they had just appeared. "Code red?"

"Yep."

Olivia knew better than to fight code red. Or at least Rachel hoped she did. In six years of working together, code red—their personal cue that one of them was close to burnout—was one thing that they never argued over.

"Your husband called and asked me to make sure his real wife came home, not the ghost he's been living with for two weeks." Rachel lifted an eyebrow, daring Olivia to deny that she'd been working like a woman possessed.

Olivia blew a black curl off her forehead. "It's just been so crazy with Frank leaving."

"I know, but you're not doing any good working like this." Rachel was sympathetic and had been helping as much as possible, but frankly she would rather eat the files than look at any more of them right now.

"Did Nick really call you or are you just making that up so I'll go have lunch with you?" Olivia narrowed her eyes.

"He called three times."

"You think you could have told me sooner?"

"You think I haven't tried?"

"You're right." Olivia grabbed a plastic bag from the bottom drawer of her government-regulation metal desk. "I've been working too much." She fished around for her shoes and finally stood, pulling down the hem of her T-shirt. "Let's go have some lunch."

Rachel swallowed a sigh of relief. Olivia could be stubborn, and the workload had been making her already fiery temper even hotter these days.

"But I am going to take a few of these." Olivia grabbed the top five files from the stack on the corner of her desk and Rachel wasn't all that surprised.

Rachel had one from her own stack under her arm as well.

Every day was a constant struggle to avoid code red.

"Just so long as you actually see daylight," Rachel said. Rachel looked down at the stack Olivia had grabbed and her heart beat hard. The top folder had been flagged with an interoffice red arrow, indicating the child needed to be removed from the home.

What is Olivia trying to do? she wondered. Olivia, after a month of debating back and forth, had decided to take the promotion into administration that Frank Monroe's retirement had created and leave behind the stress of fieldwork. Of the cases Olivia had already split up there had been no red arrows, and Rachel wondered if Olivia was going to try to take that family on as well as her increased administrative duties.

Not if I can help it. Those red arrows meant about forty percent more work and Liv had a family.

Rachel had an ex-boyfriend and a fish.

Rachel actually liked the red-arrow cases. Not their existence, of course. But they were a challenge to her, a call to arms. She felt as though she was really doing her job—catching bad guys and helping kids—when she took one on.

Olivia gave Rachel a hard hug. "Thanks, Rach," she whispered into her hair.

"You'd do it for me." Rachel hugged her friend back and followed Olivia through the maze of stuffy and small public offices toward the exit and sunshine.

They settled down onto their usual bench in one of the many manicured courtyards of the county government building compound.

Rachel rolled her shoulders and let the perfumed California sunshine melt away her tension. She hovered at about a code yellow these days. Frank's sudden and disorganized departure had been tough on everyone in the office.

Olivia turned sideways on their bench and licked the residual yogurt from the aluminum cover she'd peeled off. "How are you handling the new cases?"

Rachel kicked off her black slides and crossed her legs at the ankle. "I am surviving," she said honestly. "I mean, it's a slog. Frank really got sloppy toward the end. He screwed up some names between files and he's gotten a lot of dates wrong, but it's not as bad as I thought it was going to be."

Olivia laughed, but it, too, sounded stressed. "I wish I could say the same. I feel like I am being chased by a million loose ends. I can't even remember why I wanted Frank's job."

"Ten years in the field, you were ready to burn out, Liv."

"Still, at least it was simpler. This management thing is making me crazy."

Rachel forced her eyes not to roll. They'd discussed the pros and cons of this move to death, but she could hit the highlight reel.

"You were breaking the Golden Rule."

"What Golden Rule?"

"Mine."

"Rachel Filmore has a Golden Rule? This should be good," Olivia hooted. "Is it never, ever pay full price for anything? Oh wait, never, ever talk about family or, God forbid, marriage—"

"The Golden Rule states," Rachel interrupted, "thou shalt not become too involved." She waved her fork with a little flair. "And you, my dear friend, were getting too involved all over the place."

"Ha! Like I've never caught you crying under your desk. You've had your fair share of code red moments."

She'd had two. In six years. Not a bad average. "You're totally exaggerating." Rachel would never in this lifetime cry at work, or in front of anyone, for that matter. Any crying she did was by herself. Alone. In a dark room. She was that kind of crier. "And you are missing the important part. *Too*. Don't get *too* wrapped up in the cases."

It's not that she didn't care, or cared less than Olivia, it's that she had learned to care the smart way. The way that did good rather than made you crazy. Rachel cared with her head and tried very hard to keep her heart out of it.

It was the only way to stay sane.

"In the six years I've been here—"

"You're still a child, a baby." Olivia had celebrated her ten-year anniversary with the Department of Child and Family Services last month, which seemed to give her license to expunge Rachel's years of service.

"The best thing Frank Monroe ever taught me is that a little detachment goes a long way in this business."

"Well, maybe that explains the mistakes in the cases."

"It explains how he was able to stay in the job for twenty-five years."

Olivia scrutinized Rachel as if she was something between glass plates and under a microscope, and she grew uncomfortable. "You know, you might be one of the best counselors we've got," Olivia said. "You're smart, you're quick. You work hard."

Rachel was taken aback for a moment by the praise. "Thanks, Olivia."

"But you've still got a lot to learn." Olivia scooped another heap of pink yogurt into her mouth and winked.

I should have known there would be a catch.

"You got big plans for the weekend?" Rachel asked, quickly changing the subject, before Olivia launched into a monologue about all the things Rachel still had to learn.

"Everyone is coming to my house on Sunday."

"What's Sunday?" Rachel asked, a forkful of lettuce halfway to her mouth.

"Mother's Day."

Rachel stiffened as a cold chill slid along her spine.

"Rach?"

Rachel watched the sparrows at their feet, rooting for food in the green grass, instead of looking at the concern and pity that were no doubt on her friend's face.

"Are you going to see your mom?"

"Nope."

"But it's Mother's Day."

"So you said." Rachel fought to swallow another bite of salad and whatever emotion was stuck in her throat. Anger? Guilt? Indifference? Probably indifference, she decided. It was all the feeling she had left for her mother. "It's just another day, Olivia. Just another day."

"Not to your mom, who would probably give her right arm to hear from you. Come on, Rachel, she's forty minutes away."

Might as well be on the far side of the moon, Rachel thought, and chucked a piece of lettuce at the birds.

"Let's not spoil your first hour back among the

living with talk of my mother, okay?" she asked
nicely. She was a pro at dodging the mom questions.
And since her dad had died five years after she left
New Springs, and no one even knew she had a
brother, she didn't have to answer those questions at
all. She liked it that way.

"Fine," Olivia huffed, and then muttered *"obstin-
ado idiota"* under her breath.

Rachel smiled and watched the birds squabbling
over the limp lettuce. She threw them a piece of cu-
cumber, her appetite suddenly vanished. She wasn't
an idiot. Idiots were people who kept throwing themselves against the rocky shores of their dysfunctional
family. Trying to make things right. Trying to fix the
past. Well, if there was one thing Rachel knew, it was
that there was no fixing the past. The future, sure.
The past was better forgotten.

"We're having Nick's family and mine for a
barbecue all day," Olivia said.

"Wow, that should be quite a party."

"Why don't you and Will come over to my
house?" Olivia asked, and Rachel winced. There was
no more Will in her life and Olivia's fuse was going
to blow when Rachel told her.

"Your godchildren are dying to see you—"

"No fair using your girls as bait," Rachel laughed,
though she would like to see Ruby and Louisa. It had
been a few weeks since their last trip to the beach.

"And you can protect me from my mother-in-law," Olivia suggested. "You guys can talk about whatever it is you Anglo folks—"

"Tupperware and English muffins."

"That's what you talk about?"

Rachel nodded. "Most of the time."

Olivia laughed and Rachel decided to stop the conversation before it even got started. "Will and I broke up."

"What?" Olivia's eyes were wide. "When?"

"Last weekend."

"No del oh—"

"Oh, stop. It's hardly the end of the world." Will had wanted a family, children, a home and a dog of some kind, and Rachel wanted none of that. Had, in fact, made it clear since the second date, which was why, when he asked her to move in, she had been so stunned. Angry and stunned.

Why do they do that? Think that two months of dinners, sex and Sunday brunch will change my mind.

"What happened?" Olivia stroked Rachel's arm, and she twitched. Rachel didn't really want Olivia's pity and she really didn't want any of the pats on the back and hugs and offers of ice cream gluttony that usually came with breakups.

"We wanted different things, Liv."

I want the works, Will had said, his eyes wet as he'd watched Rachel pack her overnight bag. *Family. Kids. I want to be needed. I want you to need me. And that's never going to happen, is it?*

Rachel with dry eyes and a cold heart had said no. *Don't pretend to be betrayed, Will. You knew how I felt about marriage and kids from the beginning.* And then she'd picked up the stash of things she'd kept in his apartment and never looked back.

"You know…" Olivia looked at Rachel with so much compassion that Rachel had to pretend sudden interest in the cuff of her green cardigan. "We are not destined to become our mothers. That's a lie. You will not become your mother, or your father. You can create your own family and it can work."

Rachel sighed and looked up at the big blue California sky as if the answers to all of Olivia's comments might be there and Rachel could just point and say, "Look." But they weren't, so Rachel was left to her usual spiel.

"Why is it when a woman decides she doesn't want a family it somehow all relates to her mother? I just don't want a family. That's all, nothing nefarious. Just no thanks. Is that so hard to understand?"

"No, but I understand you're chickenshit, that's for sure!"

Rachel turned on Olivia, only to find her friend laughing. "You're hilarious," she said.

"Yes, I am." Olivia set her bag on the files between them and stretched out her legs. Rachel's attention was caught by that red flag that sat on top like a loaded weapon. "You know, I never really liked Will."

"What?"

"Yeah—" Olivia scrunched up her face "—he was just a little too…shiny. He used hair gel. Men shouldn't use hair gel. Even if they are investment bankers."

"Oh, for crying out loud," Rachel muttered. She turned her head so she could see the name on the file label. It started with an *A*.

"Yeah, he was too together, like he's played it safe his whole life. You need a man who knows what it's like to be a little out of control."

"Your insights into my love life are spectacular, really, but—"

"You are not getting any younger." Olivia crossed her legs, and the hem of her skirt lifted and settled around her knees. Her toenails, though chipped and faded, were painted pink to match almost the entirety of her wardrobe, but in the center of each was a red rose. Olivia called her homemade pedicures the ultimate accessory.

"I'm thirty, Liv. Hardly ready to pack it in."

"I'm just saying…"

Rachel wiggled her pale naked toes and figured out the key to getting the red-arrow case and Olivia off her back without having to suffer through any more talk of mothers and men in one fell swoop.

"How about I come over on Saturday and let you do my toes."

"Really?" Olivia lit up like a Christmas tree. "You haven't let me at your toes in months, and frankly, sweetheart, they look like you've been taking care of them with your teeth."

Rachel curled her feet under the bench. "I'll come over on one condition."

"I know, no dragons." Olivia nodded, reiterating Rachel's rule for whenever Olivia did her toes. Dragons looked good on some people, but Rachel believed she wasn't one of them.

"I'll take the red-arrow case," Rachel said, and watched the pride ignite in Olivia's eyes.

"You don't have to do that," Olivia said firmly. "I can handle the workload."

"You shouldn't even have it. You're administration now."

"Frank always kept his hand in. I can do it, too."

"Sure, maybe after you've had some experience. This is a red arrow, Liv. Not a truancy or welfare fraud. Take the damn help." Rachel urged. "Second Golden Rule—take help when you need it."

Olivia was silent for a moment. "You think I need it?"

"I think you're one week away from drooling in a straitjacket."

Olivia's laugh flooded Rachel with relief. "Okay." She nodded. "Thank you."

"You're welcome." Rachel flashed Olivia a smile, picked up the file and flipped through the paperwork. The nice steady hum of adrenaline entered her veins.

She scanned the information at the top of the page. "She's from my old stomping grounds."

Olivia's face mirrored Rachel's surprise. New Springs was a sleepy agricultural town on the edge of the desert. It was a medium-size town, quiet.

It was an eerie coincidence and the hair on her neck went stiff. She turned to the second page and the picture of the young girl with a sneer, tangled blond hair and eyes so angry and hurt at the same time that Rachel felt like she was looking at herself at that age.

"How old?"

Rachel went back to the first page. "Twelve."

Olivia's soft sigh was distressed. "They just keep getting younger."

Rachel stopped listening. She actually, for a moment, couldn't breathe. The girl's name was Amanda Edwards. And she was from New Springs. It could just be a coincidence. Edwards, after all, was a common last name.

She flipped to the photo again. The blond hair, the eyes so blue, unlike most other blues. Like the color of the sky closest to the horizon on a clear day. Rachel knew that color like she knew the same muddy-green of her own eyes. It was a blue just like Mac Edwards's eyes.

"Rachel?"

Please don't let it be, she prayed, and turned to the third page with the names of the parents typed in black and white across the top of the page.

Mother—deceased.

Father—MacArthur Edwards.

All the blood in Rachel's body fell to her feet and she saw stars, her skin crawled. Rachel fingered the red-arrow sticker on the front of the file that meant Frank thought Amanda should be removed from the home.

From Mac's home.

Oh, Mac, what went wrong? She shook with a sudden chill that filled her bones.

"Rachel? You okay?" Olivia asked, her hand brushing Rachel's shoulder.

Rachel took a deep, shuddery breath. "I'm fine," she lied. "I need to get back into work." She stood, ignoring Olivia's protests. She scooped up the files and her half-eaten salad and ran back to her office like a possessed woman.

Mac Edwards had a daughter.

And she was in trouble.

Rachel shut her office door and sat at her desk, rolling her chair up tight so the edge of the desk bit into her stomach. She cleared a small space on her ink blotter and opened Amanda Edwards's file. There was a shaking in her stomach, an awful quiver. A million thoughts buzzed and careened through her brain like bees.

Mac has a daughter and Frank thought she should be removed from the home.

There had to be some kind of mistake. The man she knew would have become a great father. He had been a caring, gentle boy with patience and kindness to spare.

Look at what your brother made me...

Rachel shook her head, pushing the memory to the black hole it came from.

But something had happened to Mac and his daughter. And when something happened to a twelve-year-old girl it was usually because of the parents.

Rachel touched the picture of Mac's angry little girl, tracing the eyes that looked as if they had seen too much.

What went wrong?

Rachel dove into the file, tearing through pages, trying as best she could to gather the available information from the clues Frank had left behind.

Amanda Edwards, runaway age twelve. Amanda and a fourteen-year-old girl, Christie Alverez, were investigated six months ago in connection to a fire that burned down a barn and an acre of pasture on a horse farm ten miles away from New Springs.

The farm belonged to Gatan Meorte.

Wow. Gatan Meorte. Rachel wiped her hand down her face as memories assaulted her. She would have thought that old recluse was long dead.

Amanda and Christie had been missing for two days and were caught hitchhiking along Highway 13 the day after the fire.

Horrifying images of what could happen to two

girls on the highway flooded Rachel's imagination and cramped her stomach.

Frank's notes, printed precisely in damning black and white, filled the last page.

Amanda is an angry young girl, with violent and suicidal tendencies. Her grades have dropped significantly in the past year since her mother's death. It is my opinion that the mother was Amanda's primary caregiver and when she died, the father did not pick up the slack. I recommend this child be removed from the home because Mac Edwards is in denial of his daughter's behavior to the point of delusion.

He says he has never seen her act out and that his daughter's running away was a complete shock to him. Amanda needs to live in a reality-based situation where her actions have consequences, as opposed to having her behavior excused or swept under the rug as is the case with her father. Even more disturbing, when told that Amanda could be removed from the home if he did not face the reality of his family, Mr. Edwards had a violent outburst. He broke a chair and a window and had to be physically restrained. It is my opinion that there is probably some underlying abuse between Mr. Edwards and his daughter. In light of this and Amanda's growing criminal record, she needs to be removed from the home.

Rachel had to read the words five times before they sank in.

She leaned back and counted the ceiling-tile squares, a calming exercise that rarely worked, but that she tried with unwavering faith.

She couldn't begin to picture the gentle, funny Mac she knew breaking a window or a chair in rage.

We could get married, that way you could stay.

She squeezed her eyes shut until the memory faded.

What happened to the mother? Rachel wondered. She went back through the file, but other than the note that the mother was deceased there was no mention of her.

How ironic that Rachel could have been the one with the twelve-year-old daughter—*Mac's* daughter. That night at the quarry had been thirteen years ago almost to the day. A twist of fate and her life would have been completely different.

Rachel checked the date of the file. It was one of Frank's last cases. The last time he'd interviewed Amanda was three weeks ago—the same time he'd told Mac that DCFS might take his daughter.

Mac might have run. Packed up and taken Amanda...where? The Mac she knew had no family outside of his mother and her series of husbands. Maybe he went to his wife's family?

In any case, Amanda Edwards's file needed to be updated.

Rachel should not take this case. She knew that. It was a conflict of interest if ever there was one. What she should do is march right back to Olivia and say, "I know this guy. Loved him, actually. I think. I definitely broke his heart. So, I can't take the case."

She should do that.

But she didn't.

CHAPTER TWO

RACHEL PARKED HER CAR and turned off the ignition. It was Friday, two days after finding out about Mac and Amanda, and she had finally been able to clear her late-afternoon schedule and drive to their home.

She shook out her numb hands. She'd been gripping the steering wheel a tad too hard. She had not counted on what it would cost her to drive to New Springs. Every time she looked in the rearview mirror, the scared, unsure girl who had left thirteen years ago stared back at her.

Obviously she wasn't as detached from the past as she thought.

She grabbed her briefcase and got out of the car. The slam of the door sent a bird flying from the brush bordering the small gravel parking area, beside a low brown house built into a mountain and surrounded by avocado and lemon groves. The trees flourished on the hillsides surrounding New Springs, and all of the houses along the mountain road she had just traveled were farmhouses. The file said Mac was a farmer, and Rachel could see Mac working this land. It made perfect sense.

Rachel still wasn't convinced she would take this case. She was just here for preliminary fieldwork, a rudimentary home visit that should tell her if Frank had been right. And then she would be better able to determine what to do. She wasn't convinced that this case was worth all that she had at stake. She could get into big trouble if Olivia became aware of what had happened between Mac and Rachel—it could cost her the job she loved. As she had convinced herself during the trip here, she was just sussing things out.

Rachel had gone into social work to help families. It was her job. And she was good at it. She knew better than to become emotionally involved. And without emotion, this was just another case. Mac was just another father—one who was possibly failing his daughter.

Rachel had to help. Or at least see if help was needed.

There were no ghostly remains of some kind of romantic relationship. They had been friends. Clumsy lovers and then they'd lost touch. End of story.

She checked her watch. Five-thirty, usually a good time to catch people at home. She'd learned early in her career that calling people to tell them she was coming just gave them the information they needed to not be home at the right time.

The gravel crunched under her feet. Somewhere a wind chime made careless music in the soft breeze that blew across the mountain, bringing with it the smell of white sage.

She stepped onto a flagstone path that led to the door, which appeared hidden underneath the eaves. A tomato plant grew like mad in a bucket next to a basil plant growing in a coffee can.

That's the Mac I remember.

Rachel took a deep breath, cursed that extra-large coffee she'd drunk earlier that made her heart thunder in her chest. She ran a hand down the front of her white blouse, made sure she was all tucked in and presentable and knocked on the dark wood door, which, to her surprise, swung open under the light pressure from her fist.

Rachel found herself in front of a small staircase leading down into a huge room with a wall of windows opposite her that faced the valley and the mountains behind it.

She was taken aback by the beauty the small house hid.

Pale yellow wood floors and walls gleamed in the clear bright afternoon light that filled the long multipurpose room. On one end there was a fireplace made of fieldstone and two big red couches facing an entertainment unit.

A dining room table cluttered with a book bag, homework and a plate with crumbs on it stood in the middle of the room. A small kitchen occupied the far end with an island separating the kitchen from the dining room.

It was warm and cozy, with pictures on the walls and a plate of cookies on the counter. It seemed like the very last place that abuse would happen. But that was the first lesson she'd ever learned, from her own family—things are never what they seem. And homes could be the most dangerous places on Earth.

"Hello?" she called out, leaning into the foyer. She waited a moment but there was no response, no sound, even. She took one step in and looked around the door at a staircase leading up to a second floor. Since the ground floor wasn't visible from the outside because of the way it was built into the mountain, the seemingly modest-size home was actually quite large.

Mac was obviously a successful farmer. That hadn't been mentioned in the files.

"Anybody home?"

"Hey!" a man shouted from another part of the house, and Rachel's breath stalled in her lungs. It was Mac. His deep, rough voice sent shock waves down her spine. "Be right there."

Irritation flared at her sudden case of nerves and she forced herself to relax, to remember her job. Her skill and detachment.

"Sorry." His voice was closer, somewhere to the right of her and low on the first floor. Her stomach leaped. She could hear his footsteps, approaching swiftly. "Have you been—"

Suddenly he was there, right in front of her, appearing from an unseen doorway in the corner of the kitchen. Her heartbeat stopped.

Mac. Oh, my God, look at you.

He was beautiful. His body had grown into the promise it had at seventeen. He looked lean but powerful. His shoulders filled the seams of his denim workshirt and the sleeves were rolled up to reveal wiry, nut-brown forearms. His khaki pants hung on lean hips. His hair, overlong and bleached from his days outside, fell over his forehead. She watched spellbound as he brushed it out of his eyes.

His eyes were the same. Blue as the palest part of the sky and growing confused.

"I'm sorry." He flashed his lopsided grin with the dimple, and Rachel felt her heart start again with a painful double lurch. "Are you Amanda's tutor?"

"No." She pushed her sunglasses onto the top of her head, and stood revealed and naked in front of him.

Recognition and painful disbelief twisted his face.

"Rach?" he breathed.

She was going to cry. Her eyes burned and her nose became watery. She looked at her shoes, a habit she had spent the better part of her life trying to break.

"Rachel?" His voice was strong but sharp at the end, and she couldn't bear to look at him. *You have a job to do, Rachel. Get it together.* She sniffed and glanced up, meeting Mac's gaze.

"Hi, Mac."

He put one foot on the stairs and his hand gripped the banister, as if he wanted it dead. His knuckles turned white as he squeezed the wood. "What are you doing here?" he asked, his voice strangled.

She was hoping for a different beginning to this conversation. *I suppose a hug is too much to ask for.*

Sarcasm was her convenient crutch. She knew that about herself, but didn't have the power to do this without a few crutches.

She opened her mouth to explain herself, but a blond girl appeared at the top of the second-floor stairs and electricity charged the air in the house.

The hair on Rachel's arms stood on end.

"Sorry, Dad, just went to the bathroom." The girl's voice was quiet and thin. Amanda was so skinny, Rachel's heart heaved.

Something is seriously wrong.

Amanda floated soundlessly down the stairs, carefully stepping on the edges of the steps.

She's a ghost, Rachel thought, painfully mesmerized by the girl wearing a pair of cutoff shorts and a long-sleeved red T-shirt with the name of a local swim team on it.

Amanda caught sight of Rachel standing in the doorway and her passive face transformed into a hostile mask of suspicion. Her eyes turned hard and old. She crossed her arms over her chest and glared at Rachel.

Ah, there she is. That's the girl from the picture.

"Who are you?" she asked, her eyes narrowed.

"Amanda." Mac put his hand on his daughter's shoulder, a gesture of unity and warmth, but at the same time Rachel knew he was telling his daughter to relax. "This is—" Mac swallowed "—an old friend of mine, Rachel…" He trailed off, obviously waiting for her to supply her married name.

"Rachel Filmore," Rachel said. She held out her hand, but Amanda hesitated until Mac elbowed her in the back, a little poke that said "Mind your manners." Nothing serious.

"Hi." Amanda barely touched Rachel's hand. "Can I go up to my room until the tutor comes?" she asked Mac, but she didn't take her narrowed eyes off Rachel.

"Sure," he agreed, and Amanda took off like a shot back up the stairs, her long hair a banner behind her. Rachel watched her go, then turned to face Mac, whose tension she could feel like pinpricks along her skin.

He wasn't happy to see her and it was only going to get worse.

"What are you doing here, Rachel?" he asked slowly in his low voice. He crossed his arms over his lean chest and tilted his head—familiar gestures that tugged at the lock on her memories.

"Mac, I am a counselor with Santa Barbara

DCFS." The words weren't even out of her mouth before he turned around and paced away from her. His boots clunked heavily on the hardwood floor.

"Mac?"

"I'm listening," he said, his voice cold and angry. He grabbed the plate with the crumbs on it and walked over to the kitchen sink. "I'm all ears, Rachel."

Apparently she wasn't the only one with a sarcastic crutch. She was surprised by how much it hurt to be on the receiving end of that scathing bitterness.

"Frank Monroe, who initially—"

"Oh, I remember Frank." The plate clattered into the sink.

"He's retired now and I am taking over the file for Amand—" Mac picked up the plate and threw it back into the sink where it shattered. Rachel flinched and Mac braced his hands against the counter. He swore under his breath.

"Mac, you must know the gravity of what you and Amanda are facing." Rachel took another step onto the small landing. *Just do the right thing here, Mac,* she silently urged him. "I am not against you."

Mac turned and leaned against the counter. A muscle flexed in his jaw and his eyes were hot with frustrated rage. "That's really funny, Rachel, because that is exactly what Frank told me right before he said he was going to take my daughter away."

"Look…" Rachel stepped down onto the first step and knew that her decision was made. She didn't know when exactly it had happened—the moment she opened the file, the second she saw Mac, she wasn't sure—but she couldn't turn this case over to someone else. She knew she would be breaking the rules, but Amanda and Mac Edwards were going to be her responsibility. "I can help you—"

"He said that, too." Mac scrubbed his hands over his face and seemed to be in the process of reining himself in. "I'm not going to lose my daughter."

"Then you have to work with me."

"I thought this was over. I haven't heard from Frank or from anyone in your office in weeks. I thought…" His voice trailed off.

"We've been shuffling things around. Sometimes it takes a while."

He laughed once, a hollow bark. "How the hell…" He shook his head again before looking back at her. "*You?* Of all the people in the world, you end up on my door?" The way he said the word *you,* told her clearly what remained of his feelings for her. Nothing.

"I think it's a good thing," she said in a soft but firm voice. "I can help you."

"Optimism?" he asked bitterly. "From Rachel Filmore?"

Suddenly the past surrounded them, tied them together with the ribbons of their shared, emotionally tragic history. She saw him standing in his kitchen, the sunlight casting halos around his blond hair, but she also saw him as he had been thirteen years ago, heartbreaking in the moonlight and asking her to marry him.

She didn't like where he was pushing her. She didn't want to talk about the past.

She shrugged. "That used to be your trademark."

"Yeah," he sighed. "Wonder what happened to it." Mac took a deep breath and pushed away from the counter. "So, what are you going to do? You try to take Amanda away, and I will fight you, Rachel."

Rachel didn't doubt him for a moment. "I think it's best if I review the case first."

Mac snorted in derision.

"What?" Rachel asked.

"The case." His eyes burned her with his cold disdain. "I just love it when you guys call us that. Makes me feel warm and fuzzy."

She wasn't going to let him bait her. She was used to the people she bent over backward to help being angry with her. The fact that it was Mac shouldn't bother her any more.

But, of course, it did. So, she buried her heart feelings in the cold regulations of her job.

"I think it's best if I start from scratch. We're going to need to—" She paused before taking the last step into the room. She wasn't invited, she definitely wasn't wanted. And while she did need to force her way into the family, she wasn't going to force her way into his living room.

"Please," he said after he caught on to her hesitation. He spread his arms and smiled with scathing fake bonhomie. "Come right on in. Can I offer you a cookie?" He shoved the plate of cookies across the counter toward her, the stoneware grating against the tiles. She tried not to flinch.

"No, thanks." Her cool, professional tone pleased her. "I know that you have already been through the interview process, but I would like to spend some time with you and your daughter."

"Fine." Mac nodded.

"Would it be possible for you to come into the city?" It was a selfish request, she knew it, and from the look in his eyes, he knew it, too.

"Too tough for you to drive across the mountains?" he asked, and the sarcasm that coated the question sent her spine upright. "Maybe you'd like to meet down at the Main Street Café. I think your mom still works there."

She sucked in a breath, reeling from the emotional slap.

"I can meet you here." She dug her calendar out of her purse.

"Rachel." The tone of his voice was different. Sorry. "I can meet you in the—"

"It's fine." She continued to dig through her bag.

"Rachel."

"You've made your point, Mac." She looked up and met his eyes straight on. She was a different woman from the girl she had been. Tougher.

Stronger. "I would like to set up weekly meetings. What days work best for you?"

"Thursday evenings," Mac murmured. "That's when we used to meet with Frank."

She opened her calendar and found the appropriate pages. "Okay, I would like to meet with Amanda and you, both together and separately."

"Fine."

They set up the dates and she handed him one of her cards that she'd clipped to the outside of her calendar.

"That has my cell phone number on it, so you can get ahold of me anytime."

He took the card and tucked it into his back pocket. Some of the anger that radiated off of him had dissipated and he just looked tired. And sad.

He cleared his throat and the room filled with uncomfortable silence. "I am sorry," he said, his blue eyes sincere. "About earlier, that comment about your mom."

"Forget it." She waved her hand as if to clear the air.

"But what I—"

"Look, Mac, I am here to help your family and that's better accomplished if we can agree there won't be any stroll down memory lane for us."

He watched her for a long time and she wanted to look away, so, of course, she forced herself to meet his beautiful blue eyes. "You want to pretend like we don't know each other?"

Never spent every waking moment together.

Never held each other while we cried. Never kissed. Never made love.

Those were the things she couldn't think of, not if she wanted to help the wounded Amanda. And they were right there in his face. He didn't have to say the words, her ability to guess his thoughts hadn't faded with the years of absence. Much to her dismay.

His harsh laughter cut her. "Whatever you say, Rach."

Rachel felt like Alice down the rabbit hole. Nothing was as it should be. This man looked like Mac, who used to know everything about her—every secret and longing and desire.

I am not that girl anymore.

There was nothing but black emotion with sharp edges between them now.

I have a job to do.

Rachel got back to the matter at hand. "Okay, so next Thursday I am going to interview Amanda—"

"Let's get Amanda down here," Mac interrupted. "I don't want to do this behind her back."

Rachel nodded, surprised, and Mac called his daughter to the kitchen. The girl stomped down the stairs as though she led a death march.

"What?" She scowled from the bottom step.

"We are going back into weekly counseling." The way Mac treated his daughter like an adult impressed Rachel. She didn't see a lot of that in her job. "You start on Thursday."

"No way!" Amanda bristled and turned red-faced. "No way, Dad. I am not going to talk to her."

"Amanda." His tone was reasonable and sure. "We don't have any choice."

Rachel took a step forward. "I know you've heard all of this before, but I really am not the enemy."

"Screw you."

"Amanda!" Mac started toward his daughter, but Rachel held out a hand to stop him.

"Go ahead and be mad, Amanda. But you still are going to have to talk to me." She locked eyes with the furious girl.

"I don't have to talk to anyone!" Her lovely young face was twisted into a sneer that was too old and ugly.

"No, you're right. You don't have to talk to anyone. But it would be better for you, and for your dad, if you did talk to me and you told me the truth."

"We don't need you," she cried. "Tell her, Dad!"

"Amanda, baby." Mac's voice cracked. "We need her. We have to talk to her."

Rachel walked to the stairs and climbed the first one so she was nearly nose to nose with Amanda. "Right now I am your best shot at staying with your dad."

Amanda's lips curled and she sniffed hard as her eyes flooded with tears. She backed out of the way, sitting down on the bottom step of the second set of stairs. She hugged her legs to her chest. Rachel walked by her toward the door, knowing these two needed time alone.

"I don't need anyone," the girl whispered, her words like ice.

"We'll see," Rachel replied softly, knowing the pain of being twelve and believing that Amanda truly felt that way. Rachel walked out the door down the path and across the gravel to where she'd parked.

She climbed into her car, started it and began driving down the mountain. She focused as hard as possible, with every beat of her heart and with every breath she pulled in, on the observations she had made, the rational conclusions she could draw from that first meeting.

But it didn't work.

As soon as she was out of sight of the house, she pulled over. The reality of what she'd done, of being in the same room as Mac, of risking her career for a friendship that clearly meant nothing to him, fell in on her. She pressed shaking hands to her face and took deep breaths, feeling the black edges of the world pressing in on her.

Oh, my God, she thought. *What am I doing?*

CHAPTER THREE

"DAD?" AMANDA STOOD, THE tears glittering on her round little-girl cheeks breaking his heart.

"I'm sorry, Amanda." He held his hands out to his sides. He had failed her so much and so often. "What am I supposed to do?"

The answer burned in her eyes, it radiated off her trembling shoulders. He could see it on her face, in the wild clenching of her hands. *I am supposed to take care of her. I am supposed to love her and care for her and make sure no one takes her away from me.*

Basic dad things, and he was failing.

She finally turned and ran back to her bedroom. The sound of her footsteps pounded up the stairs, then her door slammed and Mac collapsed into one of the dining room chairs like a sail that had lost all of its wind.

Rachel Filmore. He stared up at the wood-beam-and-stucco ceiling and wanted to howl. Talk about nightmares colliding. The dissolution of his family mixed with the devastating return of Rachel Filmore. Perfect.

He had truly thought the parts of his body that could feel the painful combination of lust and hurt and anger had been burned out of him thirteen years ago. But those numb parts had flared to painful life when Rachel had pushed those sunglasses off her eyes.

God. He rubbed a hand over his face. *Rachel.*

She still appeared fragile, as though a strong wind would push her over. But he knew better. Her feet were planted wide and firmly on the earth. She was as immovable as one of the trees in his orchard. Her chin was still out, ready to take on the world. Her green eyes held that wrenching combination of hope and cynicism that he'd remembered. One corner of her mouth still curved up, like the suspicious and sarcastic kid she had been, but her whole smile was like the sun coming up on a new day.

She was gorgeous and still had the power to make his heart stop and his hands sweat.

He groaned and shut his eyes. As if his life needed this.

Thirteen years spent erasing her from his memory, trying to forget what it was like to love her and for one night believe that he was loved in return. All of those feelings had come rushing back as she stood on his stairs, in the house he had built, and said she was here to help.

He groaned and winced. Help? Rachel? He

couldn't get his head around it. He'd never thought he would see her again, sure that she had moved as far away from New Springs as possible. And all this time she had been just forty minutes away? He smiled at his own nonsense, as though had he known, he would have done something about it. Nope. He just couldn't believe that she'd actually stuck around this area.

She'd said she would never come back.

Funny how things work out. *Freaking hilarious.*

What was funny was how the women he loved were always such mysteries. His wife he'd been able to read like a book, but his mother, Rachel, his daughter—all enigmas.

Things were going on in his daughter's head that he couldn't begin to fathom. Since Margaret had died, he'd tried very hard to make Amanda's home a safe and warm place, despite the absence of her mother. He raced around at double speed to cover up that gaping hole in their home. And until Amanda ran away, he'd seriously thought he was doing a pretty good job.

But now this ghost who looked like his daughter, but wasn't the girl he knew, wandered through his house and he didn't know how to help her.

Initially, when they'd been court-ordered into counseling, Mac had been relieved. Finally someone for them to talk to, a guide through this new horrific landscape they traveled, would surely help.

But they'd gotten Frank. Amanda wouldn't talk to

him. She'd become more angry and withdrawn from Mac, with his in-laws, who adored her. Frank hadn't seemed to care or understand that Amanda was retreating from her family, and Mac had grown frustrated. And when Frank had told Mac that Amanda would be taken away from him, all hell had erupted.

Mac looked over at the counter where the broken plate lay in pieces in the sink.

Way to show your rational side there, Mac thought. *A surefire way to keep your family together.*

Like a fool, he'd thought they were in the clear. He hadn't heard from Frank in three weeks after he'd dropped the "removing Amanda bomb" on them. Mac had figured they were just another family who had slipped through the cracks. Only in their case it was a blessing.

I think it's a blessing. I can help you. Rachel's words lingered in his head.

Honestly, he doubted it. It wasn't so much that his faith in the system was nonexistent. It was his faith in Rachel that was lacking. Graduation night he'd let himself believe that she was staying—that they were going to be together. But the next day she'd left without telling him, and then he made that stupid trip to her apartment, when he'd stood out in the rain begging her to come back. Although that was pretty mortifying, it was not what was so disheartening.

Rachel had run away from her family. She'd *lied* and run away from them. When things had gotten tight, she'd left without so much as a word. She'd abandoned her brother, who never forgiven her. Mac couldn't blame Jesse. He'd never forgiven her, either.

How could he trust someone capable of that behavior?

How could he trust the woman who'd showed up on his doorstep with promises to help, but who'd acted just as cold and formal as Frank, who'd betrayed him?

How could he trust the woman to whom he'd given everything he had of value? And she'd left it all behind like clothes she'd outgrown.

Mac took a deep breath and pushed himself out of the chair. Right now he had to convince his daughter that they needed to give counseling one more try.

Mac climbed the stairs, feeling a hundred years old, and knocked on his daughter's door.

"Go away," she yelled.

"Amanda?"

"Dad." She ripped the door open and then took three flying steps back to her bed where she curled onto her side away from him.

Her nickname, Eddy, was embroidered on the back of her shirt, the fragile knobs of her spine pressed against the cotton. Suddenly, Mac was nearly on his knees with the desperate desire to rewind time seven years. Amanda would be starting kindergarten, her life an open book to him. There were no secrets, no locked doors, no terrifying three days of her disappearance. No criminal investigations. No Rachel Filmore.

"Amanda." Two months had passed since the harrowing nights she'd been gone, and he wasn't any closer to finding out why she ran. "Maybe if you talked to me about why you ran—"

"Dad, I've told you," she mumbled.

"I know it was Christie's idea, but why did you go?" He watched her thin shoulders shrug. He expected that calculated shrug, considering it had been her standard answer for two months.

Why did you run away?

Why are you so sad?

Why won't you eat?

Why won't you talk to me?

Frank had told Mac that he needed to push his daughter for answers, that he couldn't let her silence get the best of him. But staring at the delicate curve of her spine, he wondered how he could push her. She had already suffered so much.

He cleared his throat and put his foot down on one side of a line they rarely crossed. "Is it about Mom?"

There was a long stretch of quiet that Mac filled with wordless prayers that Amanda would talk.

"No, Dad," she sighed. "Not everything is about Mom."

"But maybe you saw something, or heard—"

"I didn't see or hear anything!" she yelled,

flipping onto her back. Mac watched the steady stream of tears running from the corner of her eyes into her hair. "I told you I was asleep. I woke up in the hospital, Dad. I already told you I don't know what happened!"

"Okay, okay." He took a step closer to the bed, but she immediately flung herself back onto her side.

"Go away, Dad. Just leave me alone." Her voice was thick with her tears, and he knew that if he left the room she would sob into her pillows, shoving them into her mouth, probably thinking he wouldn't hear her. He had stood outside her door for count-less hours listening to her do that. *What am I supposed to do?*

He couldn't believe after all this time it was going to come down to trusting Rachel Filmore. Amanda had to talk to Rachel. It was the only way out of this mess.

I hope someone somewhere is laughing, he thought.

"If you're not going to talk to me, Amanda, I wish that you would talk to Rachel."

"I'll talk to that woman, I'll do whatever you want," she whispered, and even though she was probably lying, he felt a small measure of relief. She'd never said she would talk to Frank.

"Everything's going to be all right." He wasn't sure at this point if that was an out-and-out lie, but he felt better saying it.

"Whatever," she breathed, her voice tense with sarcasm.

"I'll call and cancel the tutor." At the moment he couldn't force anything else on his daughter.

"Okay." Her breath shuddered, her thin shoulders shook.

"Do you want to go into town with me, get some chicken at Ladd's?" Fried chicken used to be a safe bet for his daughter, but these days with her uncertain appetite and mood, he could never be sure. *Please eat. Please come eat with me.*

"I'm not hungry," she whispered.

"I'll go get some for later, then," he said, unwilling to give up the hope that sometime soon she was going to eat.

"Okay," she said, her voice muffled.

See? He wanted to shout. *See how normal we are?*

He lingered for a moment, wanting so badly to have her look at him and smile. She gave him nothing but the cold chill of her silence.

Mac turned and caught sight of the glittery ladybug stickers that she had stuck on the plate of her light switch. She had gotten those stickers for her seventh birthday and put them all over the house. *That was a million years ago.* He had scraped those stickers off his car, the tractor, off the fridge, a couple of windows. He still had one on his alarm clock. He smiled as he touched them on his way out, those faded but still sparkling reminders of the girl she used to be.

A while later Mac parked the truck in front of

Moore's hardware store in the middle of downtown. The Main Street Café, where Rachel's mom worked and Mac never ate for obvious reasons, stood next door, and the Dairy Dream ice cream parlor was a few doors down.

Maybe he'd get a pint of rocky road for later.

He smiled ruefully. He kept trying to get his daughter to gain some weight, but he was the only one whose pants were getting tighter.

"Hey, Mac!" Nick Weber, his insurance salesman, waved at him from where he sat with his family on one of the benches outside the Dairy Dream. "You got time next week to come down to the office, look over some of those papers?"

"No problem," Mac shouted back, and Nick raised his vanilla cone in acknowledgement.

Mac was upping his insurance policies on everything. Fire. Life. Car. Everything was fragile in his life. Nothing was resistant to destruction, and if something happened to him or to the farm, he needed to be sure Amanda would be all right.

"Excuse me," he murmured, squeezing between the few people standing in line at the movie theater.

The Royal had been standing for more than fifty years. He'd seen his first movie there—*Bambi*. He and Rachel had seen a million movies at the theater, though always through the back door without paying. And before she ran away, he and Amanda had seen their fair share there, too.

The cyclical way things worked in small towns appealed to him. He checked the marquee to see if the feature was something he could take Amanda to, but the Now Showing poster was for an R-rated movie.

Mac had never felt the way that Rachel did about this town. It had never been a trap for him. He'd always figured his life didn't need much more than what this little town could offer him.

He'd tried to see the potholes and the bougainvillea and the families differently, as something bad, something to escape, the way Rachel had. But somehow it still all seemed right.

The scent of fried chicken led Mac to Ladd's front door.

It didn't matter how many times he walked in those doors, he never got tired of that smell. Ladd's was right up there with the best smells in the world— sage on his mountain, his lemon grove after a rain, his daughter's hair when she had been outside all day.

The sound of a girl laughing turned Mac's head. Christie Alvarez stood with a group of high school boys. She was two years older than Amanda, but tried so hard to be a grown-up. Her black hair was pulled back in a sharp ponytail and heavy black eyeliner rimmed her eyes. Her shorts were far too tight and too short, and her belly, the last remnant of her baby fat, pushed out over the top.

He hardly recognized her. The last time he'd seen

her at the courthouse she had been a scared little girl, dressed similarly to his daughter in a long skirt, tights and Mary Jane shoes. Both of them had worn their hair in braids. He remembered the sight of Amanda's blond braid and Christie's black one hanging down their backs as they'd stood in front of the judge, their hands locked together.

God, it seemed like yesterday that Christie had played with Barbie dolls with Amanda on the front deck. He had made that girl countless lunches of macaroni and cheese and now he watched as she took a drag of a cigarette.

He was doing the right thing trying to keep Amanda away from Christie. He didn't know what had happened to the girl, but the very idea of his daughter dressed that way, looking at a boy with such shocking and resigned knowledge, made Mac sick.

Christie must have felt him watching her because she looked up at him with eyes like flat black stones. Empty. Cold. For a moment she appeared ashamed, a flush on her cheeks. But then she turned back to the boy she flirted with, as if Mac wasn't there.

Mac's instinct was to go over there, grab her and take her home to her mother. But who was he to judge? He was watching his own daughter fade away moment by moment.

Resigned, he pulled open the door to Ladd's. Twenty minutes later, he walked back out, his hands filled with brown bags, their bottoms turning damp with grease. He passed in front of the window of the Main Street Café on his way to the truck.

Rachel's mother, Eve, stood next to one of the window booths, taking an order. He shouldn't have made that crack to Rachel about her mother. It wasn't fair.

Eve, her long salt-and-pepper hair pulled back in a bun, leaned away from the young couple in the booth to cough violently. He could practically hear her through the glass.

That's the price of working for twenty years in the only place left where people could smoke unfiltered cigarettes and eat a blue-plate special.

Of course, in every memory he had of Eve she had a smoke of her own hanging from the corner of her mouth.

Eve didn't look much like Rachel. Maybe she once had before her husband had gotten hold of her. For as long as Mac had known her, Eve had been rough and broad, her eyes a muddy, graceless brown, while Rachel's had always been an intriguing blend of green and brown.

Mac started walking again. He couldn't do this. It was one thing to have Rachel in his home and in his family, but he would be damned if he'd let her back into his head.

He didn't think he could survive being abandoned by Rachel Filmore twice in one lifetime.

AMANDA STARED OUT HER window and counted her father's steps up the hallway.

He didn't even try to sneak past her room. He walked right down the middle of the hallway so every floorboard squeaked.

Three. Four. Five. The steps stopped, and after a minute, she heard her door creak open and could feel her father watching her. That's what he did these days. He stared at her as if he expected her to go bonkers right in front of him. Maybe she should do it, just start screaming and pulling out her hair and lighting things on fire. That'd give him something to watch.

He took a step into the room and she almost stiffened. It felt as if there were two hands at her back. Pushing. Always pushing.

Leave me alone! The scream clawed at her throat, but she just sighed, like a sound sleeper. Her back was to him so she didn't bother closing her eyes. She knew how to fake sleep. She'd done it enough.

"I love you, Amanda," he whispered.

Then why did you have to screw everything up?

She bit her lip until she tasted blood and waited him out. Finally, he walked away toward his room, where he would take a ten-minute shower and then try to read for about five minutes before he passed out with the light on and the book on his chest.

And once Dad was out it would take an earthquake to wake him. That's what Mom used to say, anyway, but she always said it like she wished the earthquake *would* wake him and swallow him whole.

Amanda waited for half an hour, just to be on the safe side. Once she'd only waited twenty minutes and her dad had caught her. She'd made up a lie about getting a drink and he'd tried to turn it into some conversation about secrets, which was hilarious since he didn't know the first thing about *that*. Anyway. She waited half an hour just to be sure.

Midnight on the nose, Amanda slipped out of her bed, grabbed her tennis shoes and slid past her open door without making a sound.

She held her breath in the hallway. His bedside light was still on, but she could hear him snoring like crazy.

Mom always said he was predictable.

She crept toward the front door, sticking to the sides of the hallway where the boards never creaked. She stepped over the middle stair and opened the front door with a fast jerk. If she opened the door slow the hinges whined, not real loud but loud enough.

She turned on her flashlight and picked her way through the forest, over rocks and fallen trees. Animals scattered in the underbrush and something dark and small flew by her head. She ducked but didn't stop. Didn't turn around.

She crested the top of the hill. Halfway down the other side she took the old fire road to the rock quarry.

She checked her watch again and hoped she wasn't too late. Last time Christie had already left by the time Amanda got there.

Every night she thought about running away again. Just taking off from Christie and Dad and social workers and all the memories of Mom and the happy family they used to be. And every night the idea sounded better and better. One of these days she was going to walk out that front door and never come back.

CHAPTER FOUR

"AMANDA'LL BE DOWN IN A second." Mac stepped into the kitchen where Rachel sat, waiting for her one-on-one interview with Amanda. At the sound of his voice, all of her senses immediately tuned to him like a radio dial searching through static to finally settle in on a clear station.

She could hear him breathe.

Good God, she could smell him—sunshine and soap.

She felt the breeze he made as he walked to the fridge and grabbed a can of pop.

"She just hopped in the shower. She helped me in the orchard today after school."

"Does she do that often?" Rachel asked, happy to have something to concentrate on rather than the trickle of sweat sliding down his temple. Dirt smeared his cheek and blood beaded from a small cut on his neck.

She noticed all of it in a millisecond, in the time it took her to blink. She remembered how attuned she used to be to him, how she could guess his mood by the way he wore his hat, or the way he said hello on the phone. They'd just look at each other across their second-hour British Lit classroom and she'd know they'd be skipping school the rest of the day.

"Yeah, Amanda does help, actually." He popped open the top of the can and guzzled the drink. He was in sock feet, and the uncomfortable intimacy of seeing the small hole near his big toe created a snakey warmth in her chest that she tried to ignore. "A few times a week."

"When she isn't helping you, does she come home right after school?"

"She has tutoring after school two or three times a week. Isn't that in your notes?"

"I am making new notes."

"Must be why your agency is so effective." His sarcasm was lethal. But she continued writing, pretending to be oblivious to Mac's stares and the tension that radiated off him.

"I can't believe you're a social worker," Mac said as he hitched himself up onto his counter.

"No?"

"Do you have kids?"

"Nope."

"Are you married?"

"Nope."

"Why?"

"I'm here to help you, Mac. Not talk about my love life."

"It doesn't sound like you have one." He smiled

as if it were a joke, but the bottom of her stomach fell to her feet. "At least we still have that in common, we're still unlucky in love."

He toasted her with his can.

"Would you classify your marriage as unlucky?" she asked, and the smile seeped from his face.

"We were making it work," he murmured, and studied the rim of the can.

Rachel bent back to her file. She already had it memorized, but she was shaken by the implications of Mac's obvious lie. The fact that he had married didn't bother her, but that he was unhappy in that marriage made her ache for him.

"Is that ours?" Mac asked. "That file, is it ours?"

Rachel nodded.

"What's it say?" Mac asked.

"Most of it you already know, the rest of it I can't tell you."

A smile appeared and vanished on his lean, tan face, so fast she thought she imagined it. "Or you'd have to kill me?"

"It says Gatan didn't press charges," she continued. "He agreed with the girls' claim that the fire was an accident. That's weird, isn't it?"

"Weird?"

"Well, the fire did a lot of damage. Why didn't he press charges?"

"Bill Martinez was our lawyer, you'll have to ask him. It's a small town. You press charges against two

little girls for an accident and things can get ugly."
Mac shifted and pulled a worn brown leather wallet
out of his back pocket. "Here's Bill's card. I know
he talked briefly to Frank, and according to Bill, it
didn't go well. I know he'd love to talk to you."

"Great." Mac leaned forward and Rachel took the
card and tucked it into the special pocket in her
folder. She took a deep breath; her next question was
a professional one, any social worker assigned to
this case would ask just to fill out the record.

But with their history the question seemed far
too personal.

"It says your wife is deceased," she said into the
heavy air in the room.

Mac jumped off the counter and turned away from
her, busying himself with some nonsense on the
counter, but didn't say anything.

"When did she die?"

"A year ago." He cleared his throat and Rachel's
eyes, against her will, measured his back, the curl of
his hair, his shirt collar. The handsome boy she had
made love to the night of graduation had turned into
a riveting, masculine and edgy man.

*Hey, remember professionalism? You were a kid.
Everything seems too important when you're a kid.*

"It was a car accident."

Rachel took a deep breath to ease the sharp pain
of sympathy in her chest. Mac turned again, his face
dark and intent. "Amanda was in the car."

Rachel's eyes went wide in shock. *Damn Frank.* These details should have been in the report. This was important information and she looked and felt like a fool for being in the dark about it.

"What happened?"

Mac shrugged and idly wiped at the counter with a sponge, but she could see the rock-hard muscle in his jaw. "She just lost control of the car. Amanda was asleep in the back. She says she doesn't remember anything." He sighed and looked at Rachel for a long, long time. And Rachel knew what that look was, could feel it in the pit of her stomach and the marrow of her bones. The look was about trust. And after a moment, Mac glanced away. Silent.

She didn't measure up and his judgment slid through her like a knife. It would take time, she knew that. It would take time with any social worker, but after what she had done to him, the way she had treated him, she imagined it would take even longer.

"What was your wife's—"

"I'm ready." Both Mac and Rachel turned at the sound of Amanda's voice. The girl stood on the landing like a bird ready to take flight. Her hands were fisted at her sides and her mouth was pressed into a thin angry line, but her eyes darted between Mac and Rachel.

"It's nice to see you again, Amanda," Rachel said. She had to have control of this situation. If Amanda caught on to her father's distrust of Rachel, nothing would ever be accomplished.

Amanda warily approached, and Mac leaned over and whispered, "Remember what we talked about."

Rachel could guess what they'd discussed.

Amanda pulled out a chair at the island and Mac continued his pointless wiping of the already clean counter.

"How was school today?" Rachel asked, trying to get Amanda's attention away from her father.

"Stupid."

Mac cleared his throat.

"Fine." She rolled her eyes.

"Do you like school?

Amanda shrugged, and Mac shut a cupboard door with a little more noise than necessary.

"It's fine," she said on a long-suffering sigh.

"Amanda." Mac faced his daughter with a cold, all-business look in his eye.

Rachel stood and grabbed her light jacket from the back of her chair. "Amanda, let's go for a walk." She'd jumped in before Mac could say anything else. The two of them stared at her with their identical ice-blue eyes and Rachel smiled. "I need some fresh air."

Amanda gave her dad a look that was guaranteed to make him say no—a help-me-Daddy-I'm-scared look that Rachel had seen manufactured on kids' faces for years. Kids were better manipulators than parents ever dreamed.

"You'll be fine," Mac whispered, surprising Rachel a little. "Take a jacket."

Amanda's chair grated across the floor as she pushed away from the island. She stomped over to the closet and grabbed a blue windbreaker.

Rachel followed, feeling the slow bore of Mac's gaze deep into her back.

"Rach?" For a moment the sound of her nickname in his voice made her breathless and weak, as if her bones were melting. "Just be careful with her."

"That's my job, Mac," she told him.

"I thought you wanted some fresh air." Amanda bit out the words and Rachel smiled at Mac to let him know that this was all okay. Normal.

"Coming!" she said brightly, and followed Amanda out the door.

"You want to just go up the road?" Amanda asked, poking the toe of her white tennis shoe into a crack in the sidewalk. "No one ever drives up here so it's not like we'll get hit by a car."

"Sounds good."

The crunch of their shoes on the gravel was the only noise for several minutes as they made their way up the inclined road.

The silence stretched and Rachel let it, knowing it would eventually make Amanda crazy. She kept darting suspicious looks Rachel's way and Rachel kept pretending a deep fascination with the plant life growing on the side of the road.

Any minute now. Rachel almost smiled. She would bet money on what Amanda was going to do. Some sort of screw-you gesture that was supposed to make Rachel think the girl was so very tough.

Amanda, after a few steps, pulled a bent cigarette and a lighter from her pocket.

And bingo.

She shot Rachel a heated stare.

"You gonna tell my dad?"

"That you smoke?"

Amanda nodded.

Rachel put her hands in her pockets and shrugged. "No."

"I don't care if you do," Amanda so obviously lied.

"That's good."

"Dad's so worried about me he'd never punish me."

"What would he do?"

Amanda shrugged. "Be sad, I guess." She kicked at a stone and it clattered up the road. "He told me what that Frank guy said, that he thought Dad hit me and stuff."

"Mmm-hmm," Rachel hummed.

"It's not true. Dad would never do that." Amanda's eyes glowed with earnest appeal and Rachel believed her. She wasn't sure what was wrong in this family, but she knew Mac wasn't abusing Amanda.

"That's good to know."

Amanda turned away and lit the smoke and then, just as Rachel guessed, pretended to smoke without ever inhaling.

Rachel laughed.

"What's so funny?" The sneer on Amanda's face just about broke Rachel's heart.

"Nothing." Rachel shrugged, and Amanda turned back to her smoke and Rachel waited until Amanda exhaled before she laughed again.

"What?" the girl cried.

"It's just that if you are going to smoke to look cool, you kind of ruin it when you don't actually smoke."

"I'm smoking."

"Well, not really." Rachel shrugged as though she was sorry.

"What the hell do you know?"

"I smoked when I was thirteen. I thought it would make me feel tougher and stronger than I was." She glanced up at the darkening sky, all too aware of Amanda's intense attention. "I thought it would make me grow up faster." She wrinkled her nose. "It just made me stink."

"You smoked?" Amanda looked as if she didn't know whether to believe Rachel or not.

"I smoked, I drank, I ran away from home." Rachel cleared her throat, the words sticky despite all the distance between her and the memory. "My dad used to hit my mom and brother and me."

"That sucks."

"Yeah, it did."

"Did you ever, you know, get in trouble?"

"With the cops?"

Amanda nodded.

"Yep, I got in trouble once with the cops." She hadn't meant to bring it up, that time when she'd been questioned for the vandalism she had done at McGurk's bar, where her dad used to spend the better part of his life.

"What happened?"

"A friend got me out of trouble."

"Was it my dad? The friend that got you out of trouble? He said you used to be friends."

"It was your dad." Rachel tried to be nonchalant, but she was a little panicked by the questions this woman-child with the old eyes might ask about Rachel's past with Mac. She didn't want to tell Amanda that Mac had lied to the cops, to create an alibi for her, but that's what he'd done. Cops tended to believe him, most people did, which had been helpful for her more than once.

Amanda and Rachel continued looking at each other, that first measure of each other's character, and Rachel did not look away until Amanda did.

Go ahead, sweetheart, make up your mind about me.

"That's cool." Amanda smiled, sort of, and Rachel exhaled, long and slow in relief. She'd succeeded with Amanda where she'd failed with Mac.

One out of two ain't bad for the first day.

The silence was different after that. Contemplative rather than combative. Rachel was a good social worker because she used the mistakes she'd made growing up to talk and relate to these kids. She'd been just like Amanda, not too long ago, and as long as she never forgot that, she could do some good.

"So what do you want to know?" Amanda asked, the smirk back in her voice, but Rachel could tell there wasn't as much heat behind it.

"About?" Rachel could play cat and mouse with the best of them. She leaned down and picked up a limb that had fallen from a tree and threw it out into the low-lying shrubs on the side of the road.

"About why I ran away."

"Do you want to tell me?"

"No."

"Okay." Rachel didn't smile, kept her face grave. "You don't have to tell me anything you don't want to. But you have to know what's at stake here, Amanda. You could be removed from your home."

The girl swallowed audibly and threw her smoldering cigarette on the ground.

"Is that how the fire started?" Rachel asked, before the girl stepped on the glowing smoke.

Amanda paused, her leg bent and lifting, and Rachel waited, urging the girl to say something. To be smart.

"No," she whispered. "We told the cops it was an accident. But it wasn't."

Rachel nodded slowly, but her heart pounded in her chest. "Did you start it?"

Amanda shook her head, the air heavy with secrets and misery. "Christie did. But——" Tears filled her panicked-and-scared eyes.

"It's okay, it's okay. The case has been dropped. No one is getting into trouble." Rachel forced herself not to reach out and hug Amanda. She had to keep the fragile balance between them, and hugging her would tip things way out of whack.

Amanda finally shrugged and stepped on the cigarette.

"Whatever," she said, all her false coolness back in place.

Rachel smiled and they continued their walk. What a huge breakthrough. She was confident that she could handle this case now. She could make everything work out.

The cool air smelled of lemons and sage and Rachel breathed deeply, her eyes half shut in a forgotten ecstasy.

"What was my dad like in high school?"

Rachel sifted through all of her perceptions of Mac and settled on her earliest. Her first impression of the tall boy when he walked into that consumer ed class.

"Quiet. Shy. I had three classes with him my freshman year and I didn't even know he could talk until Christmas." She picked a flat, round eucalyptus leaf and slowly tore it into pieces.

"Was he a dork? I mean, he's kind of dorky now."

"He still tell bad jokes?"

Amanda nodded, and the silence between them was like a well-worn blanket, soft and light. "When did you become friends?" Amanda asked after a while.

The chain of memory pulled taut and yanked her back. Rachel remembered the day, the moment, immediately, as if it had been waiting to be called up. "We ended up being partners on an earth science field trip. We went over to Cold Creek River to collect specimens."

"Sounds boring."

Rachel laughed and tossed the eucalyptus shreds to the ground. "It was a day outside. Your dad loved it. He'd always loved science—he used to bring all these weird specimens into class." Amanda looked at her funny, and Rachel wondered if maybe she wasn't waxing too poetic over the girl's father.

"Let's turn back," Rachel suggested, and she and Amanda turned and started back down the road.

"So what happened?"

"On the field trip?"

Amanda nodded.

"Well, in the class we got different points for the specimens we could find. And the high-point winner was this spider—I don't remember what kind it was. And your dad, I don't know if you've noticed, likes to win—"

Amanda laughed. "He cheats at cards when he starts to lose."

"I know, disgraceful. Anyway, there was this tree

that'd fallen down across the river, and there were a bunch of spiderwebs all over it and Mac decided he was going to get out there and get that spider—"

"He went out on the log?"

"I know it's nuts. He got halfway across and the teacher was yelling at him to stop. And I was yelling at him to turn around because I could hear the wood breaking, but your dad just kept on going." Amanda smiled and turned around to walk backward so she faced Rachel. She looked like the little girl that she was, instead of the adult she tried to be. "He got way out over the river and everyone was yelling and cheering, and so I don't think he heard the wood splintering—"

"Oh, no."

"Yep. Tree broke and your dad landed in the water. I think he even busted his nose."

"What a dork!" Amanda laughed and turned forward.

Rachel really could not believe how well this first interview had gone. They rounded a bend in the road and there was the house, and Mac paced the small parking area like a caged tiger.

At the sound of their laughter, joy and disbelief illuminated his face, and Rachel could see it had been a long time since he'd heard his daughter laugh.

"I guess it went well?" he asked.

Rachel had forgotten just how a smile transformed Mac. It was as if all of the goodness in him came pouring from his expression. His smile tugged at the ragged edge of memories that she'd tried to ignore. A few more tugs and all those memories would spool out like unwound yarn, and she would never be able to clean up the mess.

She cleared her throat, her laughter gone. "I think it went pretty well," Rachel answered, and put a hand on Amanda's shoulder.

"Don't touch me!" Amanda cried, all of the relaxed and easy moments between them ignited and burned to the ground. Rachel froze, shocked and alarmed. The bubble of goodwill popped. Amanda shook off Rachel's hand and shot her a look of pure loathing. "Don't ever touch me again!" Rachel staggered back and Amanda ran inside the house.

Before she could recover from Amanda's quick-silver change, Mac turned on her, his jaw set in granite and his eyes like fire. "What the hell did you do to my daughter?"

CHAPTER FIVE

RACHEL COUNTED TO FIVE. Very slowly. And again in Spanish. Two people flying off the handle would not improve this situation. She worked hard to keep the lines between them distinct—she wouldn't be goaded into an argument or, worse, a personal discussion.

"Mac, I need you to relax."

"How about what I need you to do?" His laugh was mean and cold.

"Baiting me isn't going to fix things."

"I know. But what the hell happened, Rachel? Two seconds ago she was laughing. Do you have any idea how long…?" He turned, his hands knotted into fists, clearly frustrated beyond words.

"Mac, these things take time. Sometimes they take a lot of time."

She lifted a hand but stopped herself before she did something stupid such as try to touch the sleeve of his T-shirt.

Like that would comfort either of them.

"The meeting went well, Mac. Despite how it ended."

"It did?" His handsome face was carved into wary lines. "What happened? What did she say?"

Rachel grimaced. "You know I can't tell you. But trust me when—"

"Right, well then I guess your job here is done." His razor-wire sarcasm sliced her. "You take my daughter for a walk, stir shit up and leave me to deal with the pieces. Frank used to do the same damn thing. You're all the same. You can't help us. You're only going to hurt us more."

The inner core of Rachel's body—the part untouched and unchanged from her childhood, the part born in the ugly nights with her father, listening to her mother scream and her brother cry, that stunted and dwarfed part of her—went cold. It always did when anger was focused at her.

She welcomed the chill, allowed it to calm her. Numb her.

"So go add this to your files, make your notes, your recommendations, and I will spend the next three hours trying to get a twelve-year-old girl to eat dinner!" Mac yelled.

"You are not helping your situation by yelling like—"

"Goddamn it, Rachel! What am I supposed to do? Tell me." His face burned red. "You're here to help, right? You've shown up on my doorstep after thirteen years to magically make us better, so do it. Fix this."

His shout echoed in the still air. Rachel dropped professional detachment between them like an iron curtain to protect herself from his lava-hot emotions.

"Mac, it's not that easy." Her words were brisk.

"No shit, Rachel!" he cried. "Like I haven't lived this for a year?" He whirled away from her toward the worn gray picnic table behind him. Every muscle in his back stood out, tense and tight against his T-shirt. Rachel pulled air that practically vibrated with his rage into her lungs.

Keep it together, Mac. Just keep it together.

The silence was heavy, full, oppressive. She wanted to wait him out, but she couldn't stand it any longer.

"If you can't be reasonable right now, I will have to leave and this…incident will go into my report." She hated saying the words, but it didn't stop her from doing it. "We need to work together to help Amanda, Mac. It's the only thing that matters."

He sighed and turned. Worry and the toll of thirteen years creased his face in the shadows of twilight.

"I know." He shook his head. "I just don't see how you're on my side right now. My life is falling apart, and it's like you've got ice water in your veins." He looked heavenward and his throat bobbed. "I could handle Frank's indifference. It pissed me off, but I figured he didn't know me. He had no reason to care.

But you...? Rachel?" His blue eyes burned with powerful emotions. "Your indifference is killing me."

Rachel dug her fingernails into her hand until she was sure the ground beneath her was red with her own blood. "I'm trying to do my job, Mac. And my job requires a cool head."

"Give me something," he murmured. "Some hope that you know what's going on with my daughter. That this can be fixed. That you can help me fix it. Can you do that? For me?"

For your oldest friend? For the boy you loved? She blinked and looked away so as to not see his naked soul in his eyes.

"This is not just about Amanda running away." She crossed her arms over her chest, partly due to the chill in the air and partly to keep herself reined in, moored against the pull of his powerful emotions.

"No," he said carefully. "It's not."

"Obviously, some of this stems from her mother's death."

"I know that, I agreed with Frank about that. But Rachel—" he took a step toward her "—I know my daughter and I really think something else happened to make Amanda run away."

"Why do you say that?" His relief at being asked was palpable, and she wondered how badly Frank had messed up this case.

"Her mother was dead for six months before Amanda ran away, and I swear to you, in that time,

Amanda's behavior was normal." He rubbed a hand over his face and groaned. "At least I think it was normal, considering what she had been through."

"Define *normal*."

He exhaled through his nose. "She was sad. Clinging to me a lot, but she's always been pretty attached to me." He smiled, and she saw a million things in that twitch of muscle and curve of flesh, not the least of which was the obvious pleasure that his daughter was a daddy's girl.

Out of nowhere, like a lightning storm on a clear summer day, Rachel remembered approaching her father on Father's Day when she must have been six years old. She'd had a new dress on and carried a dried clay imprint of her hand that she'd painted to look like a bird. He'd been passed out on the couch, his pants undone, his white tank top gray from filth, the sweet-and-sour smell of booze and body odor wafting from him like smoke from a smoldering fire.

"Oh, sweetheart." Her mother had intercepted her before she'd been able to give her father the gift. "Let's not bother Dad right now."

"But, Mom…" Rachel had whined, knowing that if she could show him this handprint he'd just love it and, in turn, just love her.

"Let's let him sleep," Mom had said. And so Rachel had waited for him to wake up. She'd sat on the floor, the handprint beside her in that cloud of stink for hours.

She wondered if that made her a daddy's girl.

"Rachel?" Mac's voice dragged her from that spot by her father's couch. His blue eyes were sharp, cutting back everything until just these memories remained. She felt raw. Exposed.

"Sorry, really, Mac. Go on." She felt her face burn at her lapse. She had to set these emotions aside, but they kept lunging at her from the darkest corners of her mind.

"Well, Amanda was still eating and still getting good grades, all of those things didn't change for another five months, and then—" he shrugged "—everything changed overnight. She got moody and hostile. She stopped eating. Four weeks later she ran away."

"Grief works in strange ways, Mac. She is a preteen girl, their emotional lives are about as mysterious and complicated as humans get."

"You're telling me." He nearly smiled, and she felt some of the bands of tension around her chest unlock and fall away.

"We have another appointment next week. One of the things you can work on is letting her know you're not going anywhere. Don't let her shut herself up in her room all night, don't be afraid to make her angry with you. You've got to get her to interact. She's probably developing some separation anxiety because of her mother's death."

"That makes sense."

She'd tried earlier to ask this question, but had

been interrupted by Amanda. It still felt too intimate, though it was simply a matter of filling the holes in her information.

"Who was her mother, Mac?"

Mac grew still, silent, and the skin under his collar turned red, but not from anger it seemed. She could swear he was blushing.

He sat hard on the bench of the picnic table behind him as if his legs had buckled. "Margaret McCormick."

Rachel rocked back on her heels and her stomach climbed into her throat and choked her.

Mac's knowing eyes were on her. Waiting.

You didn't waste any time, did you? The words, even though they hadn't come out of her mouth, hovered in the air between them as if spoken by the suddenly injured seventeen-year-old girl she had been.

"You left," Mac whispered, as if reading her mind. "You don't get to judge me."

"I'm not judging you." She was relieved her voice barely trembled. "I am just sorry for your loss."

He smiled then, that sad parody of a smile that told Rachel more than words what the past year had cost him. "Right."

He looked out over his trees, to the green and brown valley, like a captain looking over the water his ship floated upon. A thousand questions erupted from their buried past and brushed up against all her exposed nerve endings, and the pain seared her.

Margaret McCormick? When? Were they together that whole time? What about the night of graduation? What about me? She shook her head and ruthlessly reburied those thoughts under the heavy dark soil of the years that had passed.

Mac laughed, and it seemed so ridiculous in this emotional minefield they were standing in that she actually jumped.

"What's so funny?"

"Come on. You have to see how ridiculous this is, Rachel—"

"What is?"

He looked at her as if she had spontaneously sprouted wings. "You. Here. Helping me, helping Margaret's daughter. God, she'd hate this."

Rachel swallowed and studied the splintered wood of the picnic table.

"I don't find it that odd," she lied. "It's my job."

"Job or not, the girl I knew thirteen years ago would have been howling."

"I am not that girl anymore."

Mac looked at her for a long time and she looked right back.

"No," he said quietly, turning back to survey his land, "but you look like her."

"I will see you next week." Her words were pushed out fast by surprise and something dark and ugly that Mac called up in her, something she didn't want to deal with.

"Rachel?" His voice stopped her. "Do you really think you can help her?"

"Mac." She took a step closer to him, wanting more than anything for him to understand what she was about to say, because she was never going to say it again. "If anyone can help her, I can. I may not have lived through the same things that she has, but I know what it feels like to be twelve and so angry you want to scream. I know Amanda. I *was* Amanda."

Mac's throat bobbed as he swallowed, but that was his only movement and she couldn't gauge any reaction from that. She turned to leave and Mac didn't stop her.

MOM USED TO CALL DAD a pack rat. Amanda remembered when she would say that and it would be a joke and all of them would laugh.

Ha. Ha.

Like a family in a commercial for Disney World.

At some point, Amanda wasn't sure when, the commercial changed. At the beginning the mother, pretty and young, was always laughing. She always said, "Look how lucky we are." And then her laugh got mean and the smile turned into tears and she said things like "Just leave me alone. I want to be alone." And then, instead of everyone smiling and laughing and hugging giant mice and ducks wearing clothes, everyone was quiet. The quiet strangled the life right out of that happy family at Disney World.

Ha. Ha.

Amanda leaped lightly from the landing to the floor of the living room, skipping the squeaky bottom step.

Underneath the stairs was a trapdoor that led into a triangular storage room. Dad, the pack rat, used to keep everything Mom wanted him to throw away in there.

Out of sight, out of mind, Dad used to whisper as if it was their little secret.

Amanda pulled the string, the trapdoor lifted and she crawled inside. It was dark. Like really dark. Like the darkest dark could be if you still had your eyes open. It used to freak her out when she was a kid and she'd refused to go in there. But now the dark didn't scare her. Nothing did. Not spiders. Not fire. Not blood. Not anything.

She waited until the door was completely shut behind her before she turned on her flashlight and pointed it at the brown cardboard boxes stacked along the wall. Spiderwebs draped like lace shawls over everything, and she had to push them aside to read the labels on the boxes.

Pictures. Wedding. China for Amanda.

She shoved aside an old coffee percolator and a broken Barbie Dream House so she could see the boxes that were farther in the back, tucked into the corner of the triangle made by the stairs.

Amanda's Baby Clothes. Old Science Lab. High School.

High School. Jackpot.

Amanda put the flashlight in her mouth and pulled

the box out. She fell back, off her knees onto her butt and opened the box.

She felt as if she had a rash, or a bunch of bees just under her skin trying to get out. She itched and tingled and ached.

Inside the box, right on top, sat an old Pittsburgh Pirates baseball cap. Dad used to wear it all the time, but then Mom made him throw it away. She used to yell that he didn't even like baseball, that he just wore that hat to be mean.

Amanda didn't know what Mom had meant by that...but it was beginning to come together.

She set the hat on her head and went after Dad's yearbooks. They used to be out on the bookshelf in the living room. But at some point he'd put them in this box and shoved them under the stairs.

She pulled out the Senior Tattler from 1992 and flipped through the pages, looking for the activities section.

Drama Club. Speech team. FFA.

She stopped there and found the picture of her father carrying a box of food for the poor at Christmas. He was making a face at the camera.

She flipped two more pages and found what she was looking for.

The Science Club.

She took the flashlight out of her mouth.

"Gross," she breathed, and wiped the drool on her pyjama bottoms. She held the book closer to her eyes. She was supposed to wear her glasses, but these days everything looked better a little out of focus.

Mom was easy to pick out among the small group of nerdy-looking teenagers. She was so pretty, a perky blond cheerleader in a tight pink shirt. But talk about out of place. A butterfly hanging out with a bunch of moths.

Dad on the other hand was like the head nerd. He wore a pair of chemistry goggles and a Nine Inch Nails T-shirt. A dark-haired girl stood beside him with one arm around his waist, and in the other hand she held a butterfly net like a pitchfork.

She wore a Pittsburgh Pirates baseball cap.

Amanda checked the caption along the bottom of the picture. *Margaret McCormick, Eric Crutchfield, Marnie Stewart, MacArthur Edwards and Rachel Filmore.*

The bees under her skin buzzed louder and harder.

Amanda kept her finger at that page and flipped to the individual senior pictures. But, it read "no photo available" where Rachel's picture should have been. Dad said he'd skipped school that day because he didn't want a picture.

Now Amanda was beginning to wonder who he skipped school with. She'd bet ten bucks it was Rachel.

But there were three other pages where other pictures of Rachel could be found. Amanda flipped to the first one. Cross-country team.

She gasped. There was Rachel, standing awkwardly in her sort of skimpy running uniform, next to two other girls and the coach.

The bees stopped dead.

It wasn't the photo or the uniform or any of that that filled Amanda with a sudden stillness. It was the look on Rachel's face.

She was mad. Really, really mad. And it wasn't just in the way she was scowling at the camera, or had her arms crossed over her chest like some kind of pissed-off baby. Rage leaped out of her eyes.

Something happened in Amanda. All the things her father tried to coerce out of her with fried chicken and corny jokes unfurled in her chest. Heat blossomed in the cold, dark, hard center of her heart.

Amanda wiped her thumb over Rachel's face in the picture.

"I know you," she whispered.

CHAPTER SIX

"I'M OUT," MAC SAID, AND pushed away from the folding table. He waved off the chorus of groans and protests from the three other men who were bellied up to their bimonthly Saturday night poker game.

"You just want me to stay so you can steal the rest of my money," he said. He drained his glass of iced tea and put one of the melting ice cubes between his teeth to crunch before setting the glass down by the small sink behind him. He thought of that old wives' tale that chewing ice meant you were sexually frustrated.

It had been three days since he'd last seen Rachel, and the fires he thought long dead were suddenly smoldering again.

Someone bring me an iceberg.

"No." Joe Meyers, his oldest friend besides Rachel, shook his head and removed the cigar from his mouth. "But you have a good point. I could use some more of your cash. Why don't you sit back down and I'll loan you some scratch."

"It's only eight o'clock, man," Gary Olson pointed out while he stacked the chips he'd just won from the last hand. Chips that used to be Mac's. "You got a curfew or something?"

"No, I'm out of money." He smiled. "See you, boys." He clapped Joe on his beefy shoulder and reached over him to grab one more potato chip from the bowl on the corner of the table.

Gotta go to the grocery store, he reminded himself. He and Amanda had been living on fried chicken and cookies his mother-in-law had baked.

Not the best diet for a growing girl and an almost middle-aged guy.

Billy Martinez, the third man and host of the evening, stood up with Mac. "I'll walk you out."

"Hey, go into the house and get us a few more beers," Gary shouted.

"Your legs broken?" Billy asked over his shoulder.

"No, but your wife scares me."

"That's why we play in the garage, Gary," Joe told him. "To keep you from crying."

Their bickering faded as Mac and Billy walked to the door.

"The place looks great," Mac said for the tenth time that night. "Where'd you get the lights?" He pointed up at the stained-glass overhead lights that made the room look intimate, cozy and less like a re-finished garage.

"Lisa picked them up at the church garage sale. She said they classed the joint up."

"She would know." Mac smiled and shoved his feet into his work boots. At the mention of Billy's wife, Mac felt that increasingly familiar lump in his chest. For months he'd told himself that that lump was where all of his feelings for Margaret were, lost without anyplace to go since she'd died. But as the weeks and months since her death passed, he recognized that feeling for what it really was. A vacuum. Where all of his feeling for his dead wife should have been.

But weren't.

"You know, I must have the only 'no shoes allowed' garage in the world." Billy shook his head. "Doesn't make any sense."

"Well, it's because you're the only guy in the world who put carpet down in his garage," Mac said with a laugh.

"Thanks again for all the work you did here."

Mac nodded and shook Billy's hand. "I owed you. I still owe you."

"Oh, man," Billy groaned. "Not this again."

"Lisa fed us for months. You've been waiving all your legal fees. I just hung some drywall and ran some wire. I still owe you a kidney or something."

"Well," Billy laughed. "I know who to call when I need a kidney. Why don't you two come for dinner tomorrow night?"

"What are you having?" Mac joked. "The turkey last week was a little dry."

"Oh, strong words," Billy laughed. "You want me to tell my wife you said that?"

"Good God no, man. My life is precious." Mac bent over and pulled the laces on his boots. Part of him wished he didn't have to leave. That Amanda was here and this was their house, with the food and the garage and the feminine touches their life was so bereft of.

It wasn't Lisa he coveted, it was the way she changed the four walls of Billy's house into a home.

"So, two more for dinner?"

Part of Mac wanted to say yes, mostly the hungry part. But he and Amanda needed to stand on their own feet. The childless, older couple had been nothing but good to them, but it was time to stop accepting charity and remember how to be a family.

"Thanks, but I think Amanda and I need to hunker down for a while. We're back in counseling."

Billy's white eyebrows snapped together over his sharp dark eyes. "I heard Frank Monroe quit."

"He did. We have a new counselor."

"Who? I'll check around and see what I can find out."

"Actually, I think she's going to call you." Which would just open up a Pandora's box of good times.

If Mac told Billy about Rachel, it would be the first in a long messy line of dominoes to fall. Billy would do his research and find out that Rachel graduated the same year he did from New Springs High. He'd ask Joe and Gary about it, and while Billy hadn't grown up in New Springs, the other two men had.

Even though Joe, as the prom king and football star in high school, had existed in a whole different social stratosphere than the one Mac and Rachel had occupied, he'd remember her. So would Gary. And if those two knew about Rachel being back, there would be no relief. Mac would have to discuss her and listen to the jokes about how tight he and Rachel had been. Gary's jokes, as they always did, would turn sexual, and then life would pretty much become a nightmare.

Well, more of a nightmare.

All of that was inevitable as soon as Rachel called Billy. But there was no need to rush the proceedings.

"Mac? You all right?"

"I'm good." He clapped his friend on the shoulder and opened the door to the garage. "I'd better run, Amanda's going to wonder where I am."

"What's the counselor's name?"

"I forget, I have it written down at home," he lied, and left before his friend could ask any more questions.

He walked, jangling his keys in the pocket of his baggy khaki pants, through the twilight to his ancient truck parked on the curb.

Amanda spent Saturday nights with Margaret's folks. They were the only family she had left. Mac's mom had died when Amanda was three and his father was a myth, a bedtime story Mac had been told while growing up—a Paul Bunyan type, larger than life and mostly fiction but with a "commitment problem" instead of a blue ox.

Mac and Amanda leaned heavily on George and Cindy McCormick, who only seemed to welcome every moment they got to spend with their granddaughter and son-in-law.

Mac started his truck and cruised across town to the McCormicks' house.

At the corner of Wilson and Pine he stepped on the gas, gunning the old truck through the intersection and ignoring the magnetic pull of the ramshackle bungalow on the corner.

Rachel's old house.

She was everywhere. He couldn't turn around without some kind of reminder of the woman.

About halfway through his marriage he'd stopped being angry with Rachel. He'd figured it was stupid to carry that much emotion around over a woman who had clearly forgotten him. So he had put away the stupid childish stuff that reminded him of her and focused on his wife and daughter. He'd gotten to the point that he rarely thought of Rachel, she became a sort of passenger in his old memories. No longer the star.

Now, with her explosion into his life, everything was shot to shit.

Why was she here? She'd once slammed the door in his face and now she was back to help? He couldn't figure out her motives. He did not want her here.

And he couldn't stop thinking about her.

This morning he made the wrong fertilizer order, *twice,* because he'd been trapped in the memory of teaching her how to drive stick shift in the high school parking lot. It had been the summer she'd turned sixteen and she'd been so fired up to get her license, but her father had never let her practice in his old Buick. So he'd borrowed his stepfather's car. She'd been a terrible student. She'd laughed when he'd tried to be serious. And she'd gotten angry at him when she screwed up.

The whole time—every torturous, beautiful moment—he'd wanted to touch her so much he'd been able to taste it in the back of his throat. Bittersweet and hot.

Mac flexed his hands against the steering wheel and swallowed the thick taste on his tongue.

I don't need this. Seriously. He shot a look up at the ceiling of his truck cab. *You could cut a guy some slack.*

Since Thursday he'd tried to superimpose the image of the gorgeous ice queen he'd yelled at, over the stubborn, funny girl Rachel had been.

Mac flipped on his headlights and illuminated the dusk outside. It seemed impossible that the one had evolved into the other. The frigid control Rachel now possessed would have freaked her out when she was seventeen, when every emotion, most of it anger, had broadcast across her face.

I know Amanda. I was Amanda.

Those words worried him. He'd been focused so hard on *now,* on making *now* better, that he rarely thought of the future, of what would happen to Amanda when she got older.

Would his baby turn into what Rachel had become?

His guts churned at the thought of it.

He parked the truck at the curb in front of the McCormicks' two-story brick house and hopped out. Bugs and moths buzzed around the light over the door and, as he approached, he could hear the sound of music and conversation from inside. He listened intently at the door for his daughter's voice. Several times over the past few days he'd found himself waiting for her laugh again, wondering if what he had seen with Rachel had been a trick of his eyes and overeager heart.

So far, no repeats of that laugh. Just more silence.

"Hello?" he said as he pushed open the door. "I'm crashing the party."

The smell of tomato sauce and garlic wafted through the house, and Amanda's head popped around the corner from the kitchen into the hallway.

"Hey, Dad," she said, and her head disappeared. "Come on back."

He followed the aromas to the large cheery

kitchen, where his daughter sat at the center island, eating vanilla ice cream covered in cocoa powder. Her favorite.

Oh, thank God.

"Hi, Mac." Cindy stepped away from the sink where she was washing dinner dishes and cupped his face in her strong hands. "Are you hungry?"

The woman oozed maternal sentiment, it seeped out of her pores. It was as if all five feet of her was created to take care of every man, woman, child or dog that crossed her path. She was more mother than he'd ever had in his life.

It was such a weird twist that Margaret, her daughter, had been the opposite.

He kissed her cheek. "I could eat."

"Good." She leaned up on tiptoe and kissed him back. "Have a seat and we'll zap some leftovers."

George was already on it. Seconds after Mac sat at the island next to his daughter, George had a steaming plate of vegetarian spaghetti in front of him.

"Eat up," George said, and leaned in to whisper in Mac's ear. "Finish it so tomorrow night I can actually eat meat."

"I heard that, George," Cindy said, putting away the last of the dishes.

Mac looked over at his daughter and rolled his eyes. Amanda, her eyes so old and dark in her young face, scratched her wrist and took another bite of ice cream.

Wonderful.

"So what did you guys do tonight?" Mac asked in the loud, cheery voice usually heard in hospital wards. He picked up the fork Cindy offered him and dug into the spicy pasta.

"Well, if I intend to hold my head up in this house anymore I am going to have to start cheating at chess," George said, and leaned back against the counter. His eyes twinkled behind his glasses and his sweatshirt was spotted with the spaghetti he'd had for dinner.

He was exactly what Mac had always thought a grandfather should be.

"Come on, Grandpa, you won the last one," Amanda teased, and Mac tried not to act too surprised. Not that Amanda had won at chess—she'd always had an unbelievable mind for that sort of thing—but that she was teasing her grandfather.

"Barely," George laughed. "I had to call in Grandma for help."

"Not like she helped," Amanda quipped, and Mac smiled at his spaghetti. This was his daughter. This was the girl he missed.

"Oh, come on now." Cindy pulled the sleeves of her yellow sweater down from her elbows and leaned against the counter with her husband. "I helped."

"Sure you did," George said, and he winked at Amanda. Amanda bent her head over her ice cream with a small smile on her face.

"How was poker?" George asked, probably a little too eagerly for Cindy's taste.

"I lost."

"Humph," Cindy said, her unflagging assessment of poker night. "You want some chamomile tea? George?" She turned to the cupboard over the stove. As soon as her back was turned Mac stood, pulled the cigar Joe had given him earlier out of his pocket and handed it to George, who quickly slipped it into his back pocket before his wife turned around with two tea bags in her hand.

"I'd love some," George said without missing a beat.

Amanda coughed, but Mac had the sneaking suspicion she was covering a laugh and everything in him hit a higher note.

He tucked into the spaghetti with a sharp appetite, just as the doorbell rang.

"Oh, my," Cindy said, acting surprised, but she was a dismal actress and suddenly there was something fishy in the air. "I wonder who that could be?"

She left to answer the door and he turned on George.

"What's she doing?" he asked.

George shrugged as if he didn't know, but he was as bad an actor as his wife. "Maybe the new fifth-grade teacher we're renting the apartment over the garage to. Who knows?"

"Amanda, what are your grandparents doing?"

The girl who, moments ago, nearly laughed and joked around with her grandfather was gone.

"I don't know," she whispered, and instead of eating

the vanilla ice cream, she spooned it up and let it slide like creamy mud from the spoon back into the bowl.

George and Cindy didn't know what they were doing. They meant well, but they couldn't read Amanda's signs the way he could.

He was about to make their excuses, get his upset daughter home, when Cindy returned to the kitchen with a pretty blonde following her.

Oh, no, not this.

He didn't need his in-laws fixing him up, not when his daughter was near the edge of some unknown cliff. Even if Amanda weren't so volatile, he still wouldn't enter into a relationship right now. That was the sort of thing his mother had done, hopscotching from relationship to relationship, searching out some Band-Aid solution for her hemorrhaging life.

I won't do that to Amanda.

He shot George a look, but the old dog still pretended to be oblivious.

"Hey there, Debra!" George boomed, as though he was welcoming home a long-lost daughter.

"Hi, George," the pretty blonde said with an indulgent smile. Her eyes flickered over to Mac and he felt himself blush.

I'm too old for this.

"What are you doing here?" George asked with loud bonhomie.

She looked confused. "Cindy called and told me to come over."

"Would you like some tea? I just put the kettle on." Cindy talked right over Debra.

"Tea would be great," she said with a polite smile. She was a pretty woman. With long hair and sparkling blue eyes, she was tall and lean like a long-distance runner. In another lifetime he might have been interested.

"Debra, this is our granddaughter, Amanda."

"Hi," Amanda murmured, her eyes glued to the ice cream sludge. All traces of the teasing girl from moments ago were gone, in her place was the cold shadow Mac had grown used to in the past year.

"Hi, Amanda," Debra said with the kind regard and adult attention that a lot of teachers had.

"I'm Mac." He stood and held out his hand before George and Cindy could introduce him as their son-in-law who desperately needed a woman in his life or something equally embarrassing.

"Mac," she said with a wry twist to her lips that told him she knew exactly what was going on, but didn't mind too much. It was a twist that certain parts of his body and neglected male ego reacted to. He wished things were different and he could offer this woman something other than a ruined family, a surly daughter and a gigantic load of sexual frustration.

I'm a real prize, if sexual frustration is the best I can offer a woman.

"Nice to meet you."

"Mac here, is—"

"Heading home," he said, interrupting George's sales pitch.

"Mac, come on. You don't have to leave," Cindy said. Her eyes dropped the innocent act and said she was sorry.

"I can—" Debra was beet red and he took pity on her.

"No, it's okay. Enjoy your tea and ask George about their trip to Mexico, it's a good story. I've got some early work in the morning. You ready?" he asked his daughter.

She nodded and stood without making a sound. A wraith, a thin slip of smoke. She broke his heart.

"Good night, Grandpa." She hugged George's belly and he pressed a hard kiss on the top of her head.

"Thanks for dinner, Grandma." She looped her arms around Cindy's shoulders and squeezed.

"You know you're welcome anytime. Come on, I'll walk you out," Cindy said, and followed them down the hallway to the door.

"Honey," Mac said to Amanda, "why don't you go start up the truck and I'll be there in a second."

She darted a quick look at her grandmother before taking the keys from his hand and running off into the dark yard.

"This has got to stop." He put his hands on his hips and faced his meddlesome mother-in-law.

"I am so sorry, Mac." She patted his shoulder and

tugged on the collar of his jacket. "I didn't mean to upset you."

"You said that last time, and here you are again—"

"I know. I know I just want my two favorite kids to be happy."

He tried not to smile when she called him a *kid*, but it was hard.

"You've got to understand how weird it is having my in-laws try to fix me up."

"Well, someone's got to get you out in the world."

"Margaret's only been gone a year," he said, incredulous.

"Mac." Cindy's eyes turned sympathetic and he braced himself against her empathy. "We both know that she's been gone a lot longer than that. She wasn't a part of your family for the last five years she was alive—"

"Come on, that's stretching it."

"You don't have to protect us. We know what Margaret was like. She was a mean, shallow girl, who grew into a mean, shallow woman."

"Cindy—"

"No, Mac. I don't know why you keep up this facade that everything was okay."

"She was my wife. She was the mother to my daughter. What am I supposed to do?" They had been making it work. That's what he'd told Rachel, but he could tell she hadn't believed it and her pity had stung him like a thousand nettles.

Cindy raised her hand. "I know. I'm sorry, I just worry about you."

"Well, don't." He smiled. "We're doing okay."

God, would the lies ever stop?

"Oh, Mac. You are a good man and that girl—" Cindy pointed at Amanda where she sat in the truck, watching them "—is a beautiful gift to us and it's because of you."

Cindy put her hands on his chest, over his heart, and he wanted to roll up in a ball and let Cindy and George take care of them. Fix everything with ice cream and cocoa.

"Cindy—"

"No, listen. You and your daughter are a blessing in our old boring lives. We just want you to be happy. Your daughter is a grown girl," Cindy whispered. "She loves you, and I think that if you would talk to her about her mother, some of what is wrong in your home would be fixed."

That would be the day.

"Did she tell you we're back in counseling?"

Cindy nodded. "She told us it's Rachel Filmore and I just about fell off my chair. Is it good to see her again?"

Cindy didn't know the history between him and Rachel, she knew only what most of the town knew—that they had been best friends. So he smiled and lied through his teeth. Again. "It's great. I hope she can help us."

"Amanda seems to like her."

"She does?"

"Sure, asked us if we knew her. What she was like as a girl. If her parents were still in town. I think she got her grandfather to take her down to the café for a piece of pie, before I got home tonight."

Panic, like thin smoke, filled him. He didn't want his daughter wondering about Rachel.

I know Amanda. I was Amanda.

"Is she single?" Cindy's eyebrows rose with the false innocence of all lousy matchmakers.

"Oh, my Lord, woman, will you ever stop?" he asked.

"No." She smiled, and for a moment he saw his wife in that smile. The young version of his wife before things went so wrong. "You need a woman in your life. You need to remember how to have fun. Relax and fool around and have se—"

"La-la-la." He put his hands over his ears and started singing. "I'm not listening."

"Oh, get out of here." Cindy swatted his shoulder. "Go home."

He kissed her cheek and dashed off toward his waiting daughter.

Things weren't easy in this world; he knew that better than he knew most things. But Mac thanked his stars for the McCormicks.

He hopped into the truck and put it into gear. "Home? Or more ice cream?" he asked.

"I'm full." Amanda stared out the window, her voice dull and lifeless.

"Home it is."

Mac drove through town toward the hills.

"Grandma and Grandpa were trying to fix you up with that woman, weren't they?" Amanda asked.

"You think?" He darted a smile at her, pretending there wasn't a million pounds of pain sitting on his chest.

"Are you going to ask her out?"

"No," he said quickly, surprised that she would say such a thing. "Are you?"

He waited for a smile that never came.

"Rachel told me how you two met," Amanda said.

It took Mac a minute, but he was finally able to respond with what he thought was a pretty normal voice. "She did?"

"Yeah, she said you were a dork." Amanda turned her body away from the door, toward him, and it seemed for the briefest flash that she smiled.

Mac had no clue what was going on here. "Well, she would know. She was friends with me at my dork-iest."

His teenage years assembled in a collage of bad fashion choices, a strange fixation with black-and-white movies and a natural gravitation toward science…and away from social interaction.

God, I really was a dork.

"Did she know Mom?"

Mac kept his eyes trained on the road. "Sure."

"Were they friends?"

Mac inhaled and pretended to think about the question. "Rachel left right after graduation, so they never got a chance to really get to know each other."

Amanda nodded as if she had expected the answer. "Was she at your wedding?"

"No." He almost laughed. Wouldn't that have been the icing on the cake.

"Was she your girlfriend before Mom?"

"Why all these questions?" he asked, his voice pitched so high it was a wonder his windshield didn't shatter.

Amanda shrugged, that blithe, one-shouldered lift that had somehow become her main form of expression in the past months. He hated it. He hated it more when Amanda shifted again, toward the passenger window so that all he saw was the back of her head.

"She wasn't my girlfriend, she was just a friend," he finally said. He waited, praying for another question, even if it was about Rachel. Anything to have Amanda talking to him.

But she was silent.

He focused his attention to the road ahead with a sigh. The light from the moon filled the truck with gray-white shadows, and from the corner of his eye he could swear he saw the glittering, jagged remains of the life they used to have littering the seat and floor between them. They were covered in glass, the two of them, afraid to move for fear of being slashed to ribbons.

The idea of inviting another flesh-and-blood woman to bleed along with them was ludicrous.

It was a good thing Rachel had turned to ice and wouldn't get hurt by what had become of him and Amanda. Not that he'd ever had the power to hurt her in the way she'd devastated him.

AMANDA STUCK TO THE SHADOWS, the gray area between the midnight darkness and the thick golden light pooling underneath the street lamps. She cut through lawns and hopped the Governs' fence, while keeping one eye on Eve Filmore as she trudged home from work wearing her waitress uniform that totally looked like something out of a show on Nick at Nite. The one with the woman who said "Kiss my grits."

Eve finally turned up one of the sidewalks toward a one-story house at the corner of Wilson and Pine.

Amanda stopped across the street in the shadows of a weeping willow in the Andersons' front yard. And stared at the house Rachel grew up in.

What a dump.

Seriously, it was like the grossest, most run-down house on the street. The shutters were falling off and a huge piece of cardboard covered the front window. Eve, standing on the sagging, lopsided porch, dropped her keys and swore as she bent to pick them up.

The only nice thing was that all the flaking paint

made it look as if the crappy house was covered in butterflies.

Amanda had had two more counseling sessions with Rachel, and so far she'd managed to keep all the secrets. They'd talked about boys and school and a lot about Dad. But the bees knocked at her teeth and pushed at her skin and it was harder every second to keep the secrets.

Eve finally pulled open the screen door, which screeched like a crying baby, and went inside. A light went on in the back and she could see Eve walking around in the living room, lighting up a smoke.

Amanda laughed. It hurt at first, like pulling off a scab. But then she couldn't stop. Her chest ached, her cheeks hurt, her throat burned.

This is perfect. Like the best perfect.

She could *not* wait to talk to Rachel again.

It must have sucked growing up in a house like that. With a mom like that.

Maybe she'll understand, Amanda thought. *If I tell Rachel, maybe it would be okay. Maybe things would go back to normal.*

CHAPTER SEVEN

HOW IS IT POSSIBLE IN THIS day and age that people don't have answering machines? Rachel wondered as she listened to what had to be the hundredth ring of the phone at the Twirling G ranch.

She'd bet money the phone, which was ringing so incessantly at Gatan Moerte's house, was a rotary dial. So far her phone calls on the Edwards's case were getting her nowhere. She'd left a message for Billy Martinez yesterday, and this was her fifth call to the Twirling G. She needed information, clues, anything that would indicate why Christie and Amanda singled out Gatan Moerte's farm to burn. But she couldn't even get anyone on the phone!

"I give up," she sighed. She could simply go there in person. She kicked her feet off her filing cabinet and wheeled her chair closer to her desk. Just as she was about to hang up, a voice on the other side finally said hello.

"Hello!" Rachel laughed. "Is this the Moerte residence?"

"Yep," the woman said, sounding like Annie Oakley. Or what Rachel thought Annie Oakley would sound like.

"Is Gatan available?"

"Nope, I'm sorry. He's resting."

"Well, is there a better time to call back?"

"If this is about boarding your horse or getting lessons you should really talk to Jake."

"Jake?" Rachel scribbled the name down on a pad of paper. "Is he like the…" Jeez, what would he be called? Head cowboy? "Foreman?"

The woman's laugh was so big and merry it actually made Rachel smile. "Something like that. Here's the number for the stables."

Rachel copied down the number and hung up the phone.

The second she set it down it rang again. Of course. How was anyone supposed to get any work done between calls, meetings and e-mails?

"Rachel Filmore," she said, cradling the phone between her shoulder and ear. She scribbled some notes in her file regarding Jake Moerte.

"Good afternoon, Rachel. This is Billy Martinez."

Rachel dropped her pen and sat up straight. "Thanks for getting back to me so soon, Mr. Martinez. I expected a few more rounds of phone tag."

He chuckled, and there was something in that warm, rich sound that made her glad Mac and

Amanda had this guy on their side. "Not much time for that, and please call me Billy."

"I've taken over the Edwards file and I wanted to contact you regarding the legalities of Amanda's case."

"I am relieved to hear it. Frank was not nearly as forthcoming."

She noted the censure in the man's voice and wondered again how much repair work she'd have to do. "I am far more forthcoming."

"Wonderful. I understand you graduated from New Springs High School, the same year as Mac Edwards. I have done some research, and what I've found has caused me a little concern."

Rachel nearly dropped the phone.

"Please understand, Rachel, I mean no disrespect. I am simply looking out for my clients and I need to know if there is a conflict of interest at work in this situation."

"No," she said firmly. "Not at all, I can assure you. I am working in Amanda's best interests."

"Are we in agreement that her best interests are to remain in her father's home?"

"Absolutely."

"Wonderful. Then we are on the same side. Now, I understand you have some questions."

Every question she had had melted from her head so she stalled. "I do. However, I have an appointment with Mac Edwards in less than half an hour. Can I reschedule this conversation?"

There was a long pause and finally Billy agreed. They set up an appointment, and Rachel finally hung up feeling like a kid who'd been caught out.

She glanced at her watch and swore.

"Crap." If she didn't leave this minute she'd be late for her meeting with Mac. And she needed all the brownie points she could get with him.

She grabbed her jacket from the back of her chair and her briefcase from the deep drawer of her desk.

"Where are you off to?" Olivia asked, causing Rachel to almost jump out of her shoes.

"Jeez, why are you sneaking up on me?" she asked, putting a hand to her beating heart.

"I've been standing here for two minutes. I thought you heard me. Where you headed?"

"I'm trying to beat traffic," Rachel grinned sheepishly. "I have a case interview at five-thirty."

"Where?" Olivia leaned against the door frame, a blue-and-pink-floral barricade against Rachel's flight for freedom.

Ah, tricky, Rachel thought. *If I tell her it's New Springs, she'll want to talk about my mother.*

"Casitas," she lied.

"Yikes." Olivia got out of the way. "You'd better run."

"Thanks." Rachel smiled gratefully and walked past her with her briefcase and coat.

"I'll walk with you." Olivia fell into step with

Rachel. "What's the status with the girl from New Springs? The red-arrow case?"

Why did I bother lying?

"I've had several interviews with her and her father. It's going well so far." Rachel dodged the afternoon mail cart on her way to the elevators. "Hey, could you do me a favor?"

"Depends. You going to be at the staff meeting tomorrow?"

Rachel had missed the last one entirely. Which had apparently not gone unnoticed.

"Sorry, I was interviewing a teacher and she only had a few minutes between classes. I couldn't hang up. It was for Aman—" She stopped herself. "It was for the red-arrow case."

"Ah." Olivia smiled. "She has a name. I don't remember any of your other files having names."

"You're terribly insightful. Now, can you do me a favor or not?"

"Sure."

"Could you find out who has Christie Alverez's file? I need to compare notes."

"Sure." Olivia switched a stack of files to her other arm so she could hit the down button for the elevator. "You agree with Frank about removing the girl?"

Her name is Amanda, Rachel wanted to say.

She watched the numbers light up in descending order. "No. The family needs help, but I don't think she needs to be removed."

The elevator binged and the doors slid open. "See you tomorrow," she told Olivia, stepping into the interior of the elevator.

"Have a safe drive to New Springs," Olivia said, and Rachel looked up, startled. "You—" Olivia pointed at her, her face serious "—are a terrible liar and you shouldn't be lying to me, anyway."

The doors started to slide shut and Rachel put her briefcase in the way. "I'm sorry. I just didn't want to talk about my mom or—"

"Fine," Olivia said, "but just tell me what you're doing. I can respect your privacy."

"Are you kidding me?" Rachel cried. "You don't even know what the word *privacy* means!" Olivia shoved Rachel's bag out of the way of the doors and they slid shut while Olivia waved.

RACHEL COUNTED HER resolutions on the long car ride over the mountains.

One: She wouldn't lie to her boss again. That was just a bad idea.

Two: She would not let Mac goad her into a fight. No matter what he did or said, she would remain calm and professional. Nothing would ruffle her feathers.

Three: Mac's looks or the memories of what happened between them would not distract her. Those stupid weak moments would stop. Today.

As she knocked on the door to his house, she felt calm, professional and in control.

"Come on in," Mac said, and threw open the door. He was in the process of pulling on a T-shirt, his hair still damp from a shower, and before Rachel could look away she glimpsed a lean, white slice of his muscled belly.

Feeling calm flew out the window.

"I thought we'd go outside," he said. "It's so nice and…" Rachel followed his gaze down to the tidy kitchen and living room. "Well, I haven't had a chance to straighten up."

"The house is clean, Mac." She smiled at him. He'd always been a neat freak.

"Maybe to you," he said with a quick grin, and then they both looked away. Unlike him, she'd been a slob and nothing had changed.

He coughed, apparently as uncomfortable as she with the sudden appearance of the past. "Come on in."

It was odd how easily intimate Mac was. An "untidy" house, no shoes, damp hair, answering the door nearly naked. He was so casual, so relaxed.

Rachel had to shore up her heart just to make it over the mountain. It wasn't only the pull of memory. It was the pull of Mac, of the man he'd become, of his love for his daughter and his efforts to make things right in his world. Like the boy she'd known, but so much more at the same time.

She'd felt so buttoned-up by the time she pulled into the driveway that she couldn't take full breaths. She didn't like it. She didn't want to be that way, but she had to be resolute and strong against the riptide all these small moments of privacy created.

Part of her, the counselor part, was glad that he was so forthcoming about these details of home life. She truly felt as though she had an accurate picture of what went on day to day between Mac and Amanda.

Details like the books, lying facedown on the coffee table—one a Tom Clancy thriller, the other *The Sisterhood of the Traveling Pants*—told a good story about this family.

Frank had been wrong. Amanda belonged in her home with her father.

Rachel knew it as well as she knew anything.

But she and Mac had work to do.

"Go ahead outside to the patio, I'll bring some iced tea," Mac said, digging into his cupboards.

She crossed the hardwood floor, stepped over a pair of work boots and a book bag and took the one step up to the sliding glass door, which opened onto a patio that stretched across the back of the house and overlooked the valley.

The view was breathtaking—the variegated greens, the hazy grays. A hawk, or something, Rachel didn't really know what it was, made slow, lazy circles in the distance.

It was the most peaceful place she'd ever been.

Nothing but silence, the hard beat of her heart in her ears, and memories, long forgotten, bobbing to the surface of her consciousness.

When she was six years old her father had brought her up to these hills. They'd walked the old fire road down to the quarry, where she and Mac would later live out most of their teenage dramas. She'd stood there with her dad and chucked rocks down into the big hole at their feet, listening for that distant splash.

"Do you want to be a big sister?" he'd asked as he slipped his flask into the back pocket of his blue work pants.

She'd shrugged at the time. It didn't sound like a safe question. It sounded like one she could get wrong and maybe he'd chuck her into the quarry after those rocks.

"Well, you better get to wantin' it." He'd laughed and she'd looked up at him so surprised at the sound that she'd nearly fallen over.

"Whoa, there, clumsy." He grabbed her shoulder. Too rough, of course. That's how he did everything.

He kicked aside stones until he found a big one, the size of his palm. The size of the bruise on her back from last week when she'd left the front door open.

"Watch this, kiddo." He leaned back, his arm nearly brushing the ground beside him, and tossed the rock high up into the air. Higher than Rachel thought possible. Higher than birds and the trees around them. The rock arched across the blue sky. Rachel watched it with one hand shielding her face from the sun. The rock seemed to hang up there with the sun and clouds and birds, and for a minute Rachel's stomach relaxed. She was able to take a big breath, fill her whole body with sunshine-warm air.

Don't come down, she thought. *Just stay up there.*

But in time the rock's arc turned downward and it plummeted into the quarry, knocking and rattling down the rock face until she heard the splash when it hit bottom.

I'm going to be a big sister, she thought, watching Dad light a cigarette and toss the match on the ground. And she didn't know how she was going to keep that baby safe.

MAC STARED AT RACHEL'S back, the way her ankles and calves curved out of her high heels. The sweet swell of her hips in her dark blue skirt. The breeze toyed with her hair, and for some stupid reason, the sight of her standing on his porch turned him on.

It's because you haven't been laid in a million years and she's wearing a skirt. It's not rocket science.

But it was more than that. It was the way her eyes had clung to him for just a minute when he'd opened the door. Her cheeks had gone pink and her eyes wide. And then she'd looked at her feet. A habit he knew she'd spent the better part of her life trying to break.

She wasn't as unmoved as she wanted to pretend and it made him feel reckless. Young.

Horny. Call a spade a spade.

He stepped onto the porch and slid the door shut

with his elbow before putting the two Miss Piggy glasses filled with iced tea on the patio table.

Rachel still hadn't moved from her spot, her eyes looking out over his valley. He rubbed at his face and tried to find some kind of equilibrium.

"Sometimes, I still can't believe I live here," Mac said, and she jumped but didn't turn.

"It's beautiful," she agreed.

Mac stepped in behind her. Not touching, but close enough that his wayward mind could fill in the blanks. "There's a spring on the south end of the property."

He pointed over her shoulder, and he got high on the herbal-flowery-womanly scent of her hair. "Every spring Amanda and I go and bottle up a bunch of water. Sweetest thing I ever tasted."

Except you. The thought, like whiskey on an empty stomach, made him dizzy.

"That's nice." Her voice had a breathy quality to it that shot straight to his groin. "How did you get your hands on a place like this?"

"The spring?"

"No, all of it. All this land. This house." She turned to face him, and like the awkward science nerd he really was, he stepped back, so she wouldn't see how close he'd been. "It must have been expensive."

Well, that killed the lust in a big hurry. Everything that had been loose and flexible in him went rigid. "How did that trash MacArthur Edwards get the money for something like this? Is that what you're asking?"

A bright red tide of embarrassment flooded Rachel's face. "That's not what I meant!"

What an idiot, standing here with a hard-on while she thinks I'm a thief.

"Well, it's what you said." His laugh doubled the space between them and they were back to where they had been last week. A million miles apart. His sarcasm filled the air with smoke and lightning.

"I didn't mean to offend you." She was back in ice queen mode, her nose so high in the air it was amazing she didn't trip over her own feet, much less lower life-forms like him.

"I am not offended. I am mad. There's a difference."

He wanted to push her. Push her and break her until she bled, just like him. It galled him that he had to have this interview with her. He had to open the door to himself and show her all of his broken stuff that he didn't know how to fix. And that she seemed so unmoved, so unconcerned, when once she'd been as much a part of him as his arm.

All that piled onto the hot surge of desire he'd felt when she'd watched him put on his shirt, made him feel ugly.

Mean.

Control yourself, Edwards. She's holding all the cards.

"I worked for old man Dyer, and when he died,

Margaret's folks helped us out with the down payment. We lived up here in a trailer until I got the house built. It wasn't pretty, but it was the best I could do," he told her, gazing at the horizon but focused on her.

Her nostrils flared as she bit her lip. "We should just get to work."

We should just pretend I didn't say anything. That's what she really meant. They should go on pretending there wasn't a million memories between them.

Fine. He could do that.

"Fabulous." He gestured toward the beat-up patio set with the Miss Piggy glasses as though he was showing her a table at the Ritz.

She sat and pulled herself up close against the edge of the table.

Mac sprawled in a chair opposite her and crossed his hands behind his head.

"Fire away. My life is an open book." He met her eyes and tried to smile, but he was pretty sure it came across like a smirk. "For you, anyway."

He took deep breaths to regain his equilibrium. He needed to remember what was important. Amanda.

Rachel flipped open her file and tucked the loose papers under her briefcase. The breeze toyed with their clothes, the ends of her hair, all of her papers.

God, she's pretty, he thought, and hated himself for feeling that way.

"I've gone over Amanda's school records,"

Rachel said, flipping through her notes. "They corroborate what you said regarding her grades—that they remained high after her mother's death. Her teachers all agreed that the strange behavior started in the middle of the year."

A tidal wave of relief swept over Mac. He dropped his hands to his lap. "Good. So what does that mean?"

"Well, it could just be a delayed reaction to Margar—" She stopped. Hesitated as if the word stuck to the roof of her mouth. "Her mother's death." Rachel cleared her throat and took a sip of the iced tea he had poured for her.

Well, well, the ice queen's not nearly as composed as she wants me to believe. Score another one for the horny science nerd.

What the score meant, or why he was keeping it, he wasn't sure.

"Or…?"

"Or there was another trigger." She watched Mac for a long time, but he didn't know what she was trying to get him to say. "Did you start dating someone? That can often—"

"Good God, no." He sat back, horrified.

"Did she see you with another woman? Even casually?"

His entire body flexed, tight and hot with frustration.

"Rachel, I would never do that to my daughter," he said with as much calm as he could muster. "Do you honestly think I could parade a bunch of women through this house while she's in so much pain?"

Like my mom did to me when I was in so much pain? He didn't have to say the words.

That she thought he was capable of that, that she could so easily forget his past when he'd remembered every detail of hers, hurt.

Rachel's eyes were glued to where his hands rested on the table, an awkward inch from hers. He wondered what would happen if he just reached out his hand and touched the tip of her pale pink finger. Slid his hand along the fine, fragile bones of her wrist.

Rachel pulled her hands into her lap as if she could smell his intentions on the breeze. He snapped himself out of his trance.

"No, I don't think you could do that."

He sat back, relieved for even that small token of trust from her. It seemed he had to fight for every crumb. But that was fine, he could live with that, as long as, in the end, he could live with his daughter.

The wind gusted and lifted the hem of his red T-shirt. He tugged it back down, but not before he caught Rachel's fervid gaze on the swatch of skin that had been revealed.

Suddenly there was so much he wanted to remind her of. The way she'd held him graduation night, so tight and so long, as if she'd been trying to absorb him through her skin. The way she'd kissed him and breathed the words "I'll stay" against his neck. The way she'd arched under him and came apart like an unraveled sweater each time he put his mouth on her.

He reached for his glass with hands that trembled and wished he could pour the tea on his crotch.

"So," she said in the manner of someone trying to get things back on track, "I think we need to be looking for another trigger for Amanda's behavior." She flipped another page. "Do you have any idea why the girls would want to do harm to Gatan Moerte?"

"No." Mac shrugged. "I don't know about Christie, but as far as I've been able to get out of Amanda, no. No reason."

"How do they even know him?" She shook her head, clearly baffled.

It was a relief that she seemed to take all of this so seriously. Frank never wrote stuff down, he made snap judgments and then never wavered from that position. It had driven Mac insane.

"When I lived here, he was practically a recluse and already an old man. So what? He must be pushing ninety now."

"At least. I know that Christie got a job with him in his stables." Rachel made a note in the files. "She got very interested in horses about two years ago and traded riding time for mucking out the stalls or whatever he needed done around the place. Sometimes Amanda went over there after school to help."

"Did she enjoy it?"

A spool of joyful memories unwound. "She loved it. I wanted to sign her up for lessons, but then Margaret died and..." He heaved a big sigh and looked at his hands.

That was that. The end of anything normal.

"Do Amanda and Christie see each other anymore? Are they friends?"

"I've forbidden Amanda from seeing her. I thought it was best."

"Are you sure they *don't* see each other? At night or—"

"Well, except for school, yes, I'm sure. Amanda's grounded. She's not sneaking out at night."

"Mac, just because she's grounded—"

"You're thinking of us, right?" The words fell out of his mouth before he could stop them.

Us. Mac felt the word impact like a lightning bolt smack-dab between them. He'd said it casually, but the effect was spectacular. Rachel's big green eyes got wide and her mouth parted on a breath. *Us.*

That's a powerful word.

It gave a name to their unnamed intimacy, made them a pair. A team. There was the rest of the world and then there was...

Us.

Memories of the two of them fell down around him like rain. An endless storm of things he'd half forgotten.

The summer he'd gotten mono and she'd brought

him Popsicles every day. The afternoon he'd taught her how to fish and she'd dared him to jump naked into the lake at the bottom of the quarry. The morning after her father had given her a black eye, when every tear hurt them both like acid.

He could barely see the real Rachel for all the ghosts of her younger self that surrounded him.

"Yes, I am thinking of—" she seemed to have a sudden interest in the end of her pen "—us. As children." She cleared her throat.

"Rachel, your parents grounded you and forgot about it. I haven't forgotten about grounding Amanda. She doesn't go anywhere I don't know about. I have to force her to leave her room."

"Good." Rachel bent over her notes. "I mean…not good that you have to force her…" She trailed off.

God, this is awkward. He longed for just a second that they could both be the kids they had been. Then he could simply look at her and know what she was thinking.

"Is she coming out of her room more often?" she asked.

"We went to the movies the other night. That's a first in a long time." He sighed and rubbed his hands through his hair. "She's not eating much, but she sits at the table with me most evenings."

She smiled and looked away fast before he could read too much into her. "That's improvement."

"Well," he scoffed, "sort of."

"These things—"

"Take time," he finished for her. "I think I've heard that one before. I want to take her camping next weekend." She looked up fast and their eyes finally collided. They'd camped a lot together. Suddenly the seams between them pulled tight and he wanted her to talk to him. But there was still so much in the way. The past. Amanda.

"Camping would be good," she said with a smile. "It's been a long time since I slept outside."

He smiled, caught for a moment in their shared past. "Remember Jesse?" he asked, and her eyelids flinched at her little brother's name.

"Of course," she replied, but did not look up.

"No, I mean the time your parents grounded him from hanging out with us. We were going camping. Remember? We were, like, sixteen. And by the time we got to the quarry your brother was already there."

"I remember."

"He already had that fire burning. He must have gotten grounded and turned right around for the quarry. He was such a little shit."

"That was Jesse." Her hands trembled as she put down her pen. He could practically see the cracks in her icy veneer and he knew he should let up. Drop the subject, but he didn't want to. It felt so good to remind her of all the things she tried so hard to forget.

"I'm sorry, I shouldn't have said anything," he apologized.

"No, it's fine." Her smile was fake and it lit a match to his blood.

"How is Jesse doing?" Mac asked, knowing she didn't know, but relishing the fact that her private life was no prize, either. Her closets were filled with just as many skeletons as his own.

"He's good."

"Where is he?"

She slammed her notebook shut. "What do you want me to say, Mac? He's in the army. That's all I know."

"He fell apart when you left." All the color drained from her face. She blinked rapidly, but the bright haze of tears lingered.

Every nerve ending thrummed. Sparks practically filled the air when their eyes met and clashed. Through the film of tears he saw her anger and her strength of will, and, again, that look of hers went through him like an electrical current.

But then she blinked, the tears vanished and the electricity died.

"You just want to watch me squirm, Mac. And I won't be manipulated—"

"One night when Jesse was sixteen, he hit your father back. I had to bail him out—" He ignored her, pressed harder. Dug deeper for that glimpse of humanity he just saw.

Rachel leaped from her seat, her patio chair scraping across the wood of the deck.

Mac stood, too. "You could have written. You could have tried—"

"You think I didn't?" she cried. Rachel stepped away from the table, but Mac lifted his hand as though he was going to grab her arm. They both went still as if waiting for that touch.

Do it. Touch her. Watch what happens.

But he wasn't an idiot.

He dropped his hand and Rachel sucked in air.

"You wrote to him?"

She remained silent, staring off into the middle distance between them.

"Rach?"

"Every week," she said. "Every week until last year when he finally wrote back and told me to stop."

Mac recognized the grief in the endless green depths of her beautiful eyes. Suddenly he knew this woman standing across from him. He saw his old friend in her trembling lips and the stubborn set of her chin. The way she fought tears as if her life depended on it.

Oh, God. I missed you. He didn't say it, but the thought filled him like fresh, sweet water, and for the first time since Rachel had walked in the door, he wondered if maybe they would make it.

"I'm sorry. Jesse was very…angry. For years."

"You stayed friends?" Her voice was barely audible, carried on the wind rushing up from the valley.

Mac smiled. "I don't know if I would say *friends*, exactly. I bailed him out of jail. I gave him work when he needed it. I helped him bury your dad, watched him cry while he did it. I saw him off at the train station when he left for basic training."

"I'm glad." She managed to smile and it broke his heart. "He always liked you."

"He loved you."

Acid tinged her laughter. "Right. Look how well I did with that."

He stepped around the table toward her. Moving as slowly as possible. She was like a deer who would bolt at any moment. He was so close. They were so close to having the puzzle fit together.

"You know, it took me a long time to figure you out when we were growing up. You talked so tough, but you weren't kidding anyone, least of all me. But I couldn't figure out why. Why pretend to be so tough." He was talking about her as an adult, the way she was right now, and they both knew it.

He counted her breaths, her heartbeat in her throat, the slow blinks of her eyelashes.

"So, have you?" she whispered. "Figured me out?"

CHAPTER EIGHT

"YES, I THINK SO," MAC SMILED and prepared to welcome his old friend Rachel back into his life.

"This should be good."

He ignored her sarcasm, dismissing it as a product of the fake Ice Queen Rachel. He leaned in, willing her to remember their friendship. "It's because it hurt so much when we were kids and it still hurts."

"What does?"

"Hoping things will be different. That you can make them different."

Rachel flinched as if he'd slapped her and started to stack her notebook and file.

He'd lost her. He'd pushed too hard.

Damn it.

"I don't think about the past much, to be honest," she obviously lied. "We either discuss the case, or there is nothing for us to talk about. Now, what do you want to do?"

"Rachel, I was there. You don't have to pretend." He verbally scrambled to get back to the moment they'd just shared, the moment when he thought he'd touched her.

"Pretend what?" Her words gave him frostbite. "I am just trying to help you with your daughter, which obviously you don't need, since you'd rather talk about anything other than your daughter." When she looked at him, he didn't know who she was. Her eyes were empty.

"You know that's not true, but I can't pretend we don't know each other."

"You said you could."

"I was wrong—" Before the words were even out of his mouth, she turned and opened the door and stepped into the house.

"Rachel, stop!"

"I will see you next week," she called over her shoulder in her quick retreat to the front door. "And by then maybe you can forget this crusade to hurt me and get back to business."

"Rachel! Don't leave like this."

They didn't have time to play these games. His daughter was fading into dust in front of his eyes and Rachel was supposed to help, damn it. And she kept running every time things got uncomfortable.

He darted from the back door to the front and stood in her way.

"I am treating you with professionalism," she bit out. "I would appreciate the same."

"We have a past, Rachel. And I won't—"

"The past has nothing to do with this. I told you that before. I am here to help you and your daughter—"

"Why?"

The question stalled her. "Why what?"

"Why did you take our case? I can't figure it out. I'm fairly sure you're breaking all kinds of rules considering how we knew each other."

"That's my point, Mac. Without our past I am just a counselor trying to help a family going through a rough time."

How could she turn herself off like that? A minute ago she was on the verge of tears and now she might as well be taking his lunch order.

"What the hell happened to you, Rach? You are some kind of ice sculpture. You don't have a pulse."

"Get out of my way."

He ached to touch her, to see if she was as cold as she seemed.

Instead of moving away, he leaned closer until her breath fanned his cheek and he could smell her perfume, a mystery aroma that seemed to well up from the shadow between her breasts.

"We are our past," he whispered. "All the shit you want to ignore is what makes us who we are. And you are forgetting the fact that I had a front-row seat for everything that happened to you."

"I have put the past behind me." Every word was a sharp dagger she slashed at him.

"Come on, look at what you do for a living."

"What do you mean by that?"

"Are you trying to say that you don't see your job as a way to make up for your past, a way to change what happened?"

"Absolutely not. It's a way to make sure it never happens again. It's a way to bury it and move on."

"Is that why you're here? To bury me and move on?"

"Mac—" she stepped even closer "—I buried you thirteen years ago. Don't you remember?"

Mac's stomach went cold. His face hot. Her words were poison entering his bloodstream. It hurt so much he wanted to laugh. He wanted to grip his chest and howl. *How is it possible that she can still hurt me?*

Her eyes were wide and shocked over the hand she put to her lips as if to stop more poison from leaking out.

The worst parts of him seethed. Anger and pettiness and low impulses boiled over and he opened his mouth to let her have it.

"Stop." She held up a trembling hand. "Just stop. We can't keep doing this, Mac. We're acting like children."

He bit his tongue and didn't say anything. It was so like her to annihilate him with perfectly hurtful words, then raise her hand and call foul.

"I want to help. I do. But we're making things worse arguing like this." Her voice was unsteady and two bright red spots burned on her cheeks. "We need to find a solution to this…issue between us."

Issue. Oh, that's a good one.

"I spent at least four years after you left imagining all the things that I would say to you if I could," he told her, pleased when she licked her lips and looked anxious.

"Do you want to do that now?" she whispered.

"No. I got over you a long time ago." The hectic spots of color on her cheeks spread down to her neck and chest, and he studied her skin as though it was a map and he was lost in the desert.

"That's good." She nodded. "We can build on that."

"It doesn't change the fact that I don't trust you."

Her eyes, surprised and wary, met his. He had chosen his words carefully. He wanted to take her apart with surgical skill. Leave her in the same shambles she'd left him.

"You run from everything. You ran from your family and from me. You're running now. I'm scared you might run when my daughter and I need you the most."

"Mac, we were kids. If you can't forget—"

"I'm not done." His voice rose in volume. "You were right when you said that you know my daughter. She's just like you were."

"So?"

"I'm worried Amanda will turn out like you. And the idea makes me sick."

Rachel took a half step backward. She bowed her head and touched her temple with her fingers. More than anything Mac wished that he felt good about what he'd just said. But he didn't.

He felt hollow.

"Rach—"

"I'll resign from the case tomorrow." She shook her hair away from her pale face. "You'll be assigned a new counselor by the end of the month."

She hiked her briefcase over her shoulder and walked past him.

"Rachel!" He'd screwed up. Again. That was wrong thing to do. He should have played by her frigid rules. "Rach. Come back—"

She ignored him. Walked faster. Left him behind.

Mac closed his eyes and swore. He banged the side of his head against the open door. "You. Are. So. Stupid."

"Dad?"

Mac's heart stopped and he turned to face his daughter where she sat at the old picnic table under the eaves.

"Amanda, what are you doing here?" *Oh, God, did she hear that? Of course she heard it. She's three feet away.* "I thought you were with Grandma."

"She dropped me off a little while ago."

Oh. No. "Why didn't you come tell me?"

She shrugged, kicked at a rock.

"Did you—" he swallowed "—hear any of that?"

She nodded.

"Amanda, oh sweetheart, I'm sorry. I just—"

"She's not coming back?" Amanda pointed at the dust that still hung in the air from Rachel's retreat.

"I don't think so. But don't worry, we're going to be okay. We'll get a new counselor." Mac took a step toward her and Amanda, his baby, the only reason he had to live these days, flinched.

"Why'd you say those things?" she asked, her voice low and hot as if it was born in some pit of coals in her body. "Why'd you have to be so mean to her?"

"Sweetheart, you don't understand."

Amanda started laughing, but it came out sounding broken. "*You* don't get it, Dad. You never get it."

"Then help me," he pleaded. "What is it? Is it me? Is it mom? Is it—"

"It's Rachel."

Mac rocked back on his heels. All he could do was blink.

"You want Rachel back? But you were so mad after your meeting. I didn't think you would—" He stopped talking. He was out of breath. Out of options. "You really want her back?"

Normally the small nod of Amanda's head wouldn't even be noticeable, but she held herself so supernaturally still that Mac could see the beat of her heart in her temple. When she nodded it was as good as a scream.

"Okay," he breathed. "Okay we'll get her back."

"You're going to be too late," Amanda sneered,

seconding Mac's own thoughts. "You were mean. If I were her, I wouldn't ever talk to you again."

She walked past him, straight up the stairs to her room.

Mac could only watch her go, unsure if what just happened was a good thing or the worst possible turn of events excluding nuclear disaster.

Right now his money was on nuclear disaster.

CHAPTER NINE

RACHEL YANKED ON THE back door's rusty, broken handle, but it didn't budge. Dad had locked her out again.

Asshole. She could hear them inside, yelling at each other.

"You're going to wake Jesse!" screamed Mom in a voice that could break glass on the other side of town.

"This is my house!" her father screamed back, his old argument-ender. *My house. My rules. Obey them or get the snot punched out of you.*

Rachel wished she could run in there and tell her mother to leave it alone. To walk away before he hit her.

Rachel yanked on the handle again, rattling the beat-up aluminum door on its hinges.

Inside, something smashed followed by a terrible ugly moment of silence. Did he finally do it this time? Had he killed her? Was Mom bleeding to death on the floor while Dad looked around for his beer and the remote control?

Rachel held her breath.

Please. Please. Please. What she was praying for she couldn't even say.

"Goddamn it, Mick! You broke the lamp!" Mom screamed, and Rachel sagged in relief, held up by the screen door.

Galvanized by fear and anger, Rachel ran around to the other side of the house. She stepped into the flower bed of overgrown weeds and roses. The thorns snagged her jeans and the skin of her arms but she ignored the pricks of pain.

She stood on tiptoe and hopped until she knocked on the glass of Jesse's window. She did it again. And again until finally she heard someone moving around inside. The window slid up and her brother peered over the sill.

"Hey," she said, and stumbled back through the thorns into the messy yard so she wouldn't have to stare straight up to see him.

"What are you doing?" he asked, rubbing his eyes. "It's the middle of the night."

His short black hair stood up in a rooster tail on the top of his head and the breeze made the strands bob. She could see the ragged red collar of his favorite superhero pyjamas.

"We gotta go. Can you climb down?"

"Go where? It's so dark out, Rach."

"Yeah, I know, buddy, but that's the best time to get away. Come on, can't you hear Mom and Dad yelling?"

There was another tremendous smash and Jesse

looked over his shoulder. "I'm scared. You come in!" He turned back to her and reached out with his little-boy arms. "Climb in through the window."

"Yeah, Rachel." Another pair of arms stretched out the window as Mac emerged from the shadows to stand next to Jesse. His white-blond hair glowed like bone in the moonlight. "Come on, I'll help you." He reached out farther, almost touched her hair, her face….

Rachel sat up with a jerk. Knocked the bedcovers onto her bedside lamp and it rattled like a locked aluminum door.

"Mac?" she cried, searching the shadows. "Jesse? Where are you?"

The shadows shifted and lights made tracks across her ceiling as another truck passed the road outside her house.

My house.

She flopped back on her bed and took deep breaths until she could think over the pounding of the blood in her brain.

The passing truck was long gone and the emptiness of the small room was once again familiar. Not filled with comforting mementos and souvenirs from easier times. Not homey or pretty. Just familiar.

And at some point in the passing years that had become enough for her.

Familiar.

Damn Mac. Damn him for bringing this crap up. She hadn't had a nightmare in years. She'd been able to put Jesse away, lock him in the box that held all the things in her life that had gone wrong but couldn't be changed.

She couldn't do this. Couldn't survive these nightmares and the guilt and the worry again.

She reached for the sheets she'd kicked off and knocked over the empty wineglass she had set on the floor before going to bed.

The wine, even just the one glass, had been a decidedly bad idea.

No wonder I'm having nightmares. She picked up the wineglass and walked out of her bedroom into her dark hallway to the kitchen. The bright waning moon filled her small bungalow with enough light that she didn't need any lamps. Which was good. The dark suited her.

The cool counter bit into her side when she leaned against it and she welcomed the chill and discomfort. Wanted it.

Just as she had wanted the wine. Just as she had wanted to keep driving away from Mac. Not stopping until she got to Alaska—someplace cold enough to send her emotions back into deep freeze.

You're like an ice sculpture. You don't have a pulse.

She wished she could rail against Mac's accusations. Call him a liar and tell him he didn't know what he was talking about. But Mac was right. The things he'd said were true.

She was frozen so she wouldn't hurt.

She closed her eyes against the hot burn of tears. *Goddamn it, Mac.*

Had she made mistakes? In her efforts to protect the remaining pieces of herself, had she done all the wrong things?

If she had stayed in New Springs, would she be happier now? Would she spend Mother's Day with her mother rather than with her boss? Would she be with Mac? It was some sick joke that no man, no boyfriend, no lover, no other friend had ever understood her, or cared for her the way he did. Not even Olivia.

And it wasn't just the intimacy of the past that they shared. It was her body and the way it shivered, constricted and warmed at the sight of him.

She filled up a water glass and drank it down. She wiped the sudden sweat off her forehead. She was parched. Drying up. She ran cold water over her wrists, splashed it on her face, licked it off her lips.

What is happening to me?

And now Mac was gone—again. And she felt as she had thirteen years ago, bereft and angry. Which was ridiculous since she'd done the leaving both times.

She leaned against the counter, rested her head against the cupboards.

"What have I done?" she whispered.

You've abandoned your brother. You've run from your family. You've broken your best friend's heart and you've deserted a little girl who needs you. Nice job, counselor.

Suddenly, more than anything she wanted to change one of those things. Just one. Prove Mac wrong. She wasn't inhuman and uncaring.

The impulse bit hard into her belly and she couldn't shake it. She nearly groaned, torn inside from what she wanted and what she had.

Do something right. Make something better.

It's all she'd ever wanted to do. Her whole life. But her father's drinking and her mother's enabling had been mountains too big for her to climb on her own.

She'd tried and she'd fallen a million times. She could never be good enough for her father. She could never convince her mother to leave him. She could never protect her brother. The best she could do was to try to protect other kids.

Mac was right.

She clapped a hand over her hysterical laugh. She was a DCFS employee because she was still trying to fix her family.

Every kid was her brother. Every kid was her. Every abusive or neglectful parent was her own.

She pushed away from the counter and headed back to her bedroom. She flicked on the light and blinked at the brightness.

She opened her closet and pulled out the boxes of shoes on the shelf without any care. Boxes hit the carpet and high heels spilled out around her. Finally, in the far back corner she found her old army-green backpack.

She yanked it down and sat on the rug beside her bed.

Rachel traced the curled-up edges of the Earth Day patches she'd sewed on the bag to cover up the holes. She smiled at the Nine Inch Nails buttons that festooned the small pocket in front. She'd never really liked the band, but Mac had adored them.

His iced tea addiction wasn't the only indication of their friendly compromises.

She opened up the bag and pulled out all of the letters stamped Return to Sender that she kept in the bag. Dozens of them. Jesse hadn't sent every letter back. Some she didn't know if he'd kept or never received. But about one in three of the hundreds she'd mailed ended up back to her.

Just looking at his name in her handwriting filled her throat with thick pain.

At the bottom of the bag was a small Hello Kitty box filled with paper, envelopes, stamps and pens. It had been her stationery box when she was a kid, a gift from a grandmother she rarely saw. She had no clue why she kept it, or why she still used it to store her paper. Well, that wasn't true. She did know. She just hated what it said about herself. She kept this box and these letters locked up, put away in a child's bag, as far from her current life as possible.

And never the two shall meet.

Except for nights such as this one, when the

abyss that her childhood had carved into her was one small step away.

She opened the box. Pulled out a pen and a piece of pale ivory paper, set the box on her knees with the paper draped over it and began to write.

Jesse,
I am sorry. I didn't know what I was supposed to do thirteen years ago. I still don't. I was just a kid and our house was so bad that I thought if I left, maybe it wouldn't be that bad anymore. Maybe he wouldn't scream and, without me to hit, maybe he wouldn't hit. All I knew for sure was that if I left, things would be better for me and at that time, that's all I cared about. I know how selfish that sounds and if I could change it, I would. In a heartbeat. I don't blame you for being angry—I would be, too. At least we have that in common—both of us think I'm a terrible sister. But I want to make up for what I did. For the years that we've wasted. I know you told me not to write, but all I've got of you are these dumb letters that hopefully you read. So, I'm going to keep writing, because it's too hard not to.
I miss you, Jesse. And I know you don't believe it, but I love you.

She signed it. Shoved it in an envelope, put two stamps on the thing because prices had gone up since she'd bought these ones and addressed it Private Jesse Filmore at the San Diego Army Base.

He probably wasn't there anymore. Could, in fact, be in Iraq and she wouldn't know. She put her hands to her face, biting back sudden tears.

He could be dead and she wouldn't know.

She took a deep breath and pulled herself away from that thought. Her mother would have contacted her if Jesse had died. Wouldn't she?

She stroked a Nine Inch Nails button. *No, Mom wouldn't.* Rachel had cut those ties.

Tomorrow morning she was going to resign from Mac's case, something that felt wrong in the marrow of her bones. But she didn't have much of a choice. Mac hated her and she couldn't blame him.

But this, she pressed the letter to her lips, *this feels right.*

MAC JERKED AWAKE WHEN HIS book hit his nose. Hard.

"Ouch," he muttered, rubbing his face. "Why do I even bother." He thumb-eared his page, the same page he'd thumb-eared last night, and slid the book onto his nightstand before pulling the chain on his bedside lamp.

The waning moon hung in a clear black sky and filled his bedroom with bright white light. The landscape of his room—the armoire, the chair covered in his clothes, Margaret's old dresser, all the things so familiar to him he barely saw them anymore—was changed. Made new and different.

He lifted his hands so the white light seemed to pool in his palms. All the cuts and scrapes and bruises of his occupation that marred his rough skin were invisible in the bleached-out illumination.

He had the hands of a young man.

And suddenly, there it was, the memory he had spent so many years pushing away and ignoring.

The shadows of his bedroom changed into the rock quarry. And the young hands in front of him were not the trick of lighting, they were his. A seventeen-year-old, freshly graduated from high school version of him.

He closed his eyes. Tried to think of accounting. The bug problem on the lower acreage. The lemons he needed to harvest. But none of it worked.

Alone in the quiet stillness of his room, things he'd been sure were left behind, or burned out of him by anger and humiliation, exploded in his mind.

The way Rachel's skin had turned to pearl in the moonlight. The soft warm silk of her breasts, her waist. The moist heat of her breath against his cheek, his name a sigh on her lips. The slick, tight heat of her body. Her gasp of pain and the bright banner of blood on his penis when it was all over.

They had both been virgins. Her more so than him, thanks to the science tutoring he'd given Margaret. But that night had been the perfect culmination of everything he'd felt for Rachel. He'd been convinced as he'd stroked her stomach and kissed her breasts that she was his soul mate.

Now he was thirty, a father, a widower, no longer a boy. But heat still coiled in his belly, spread down into his groin.

You are one lonely man.

But he couldn't tease or shame himself out of his mood. The memory clung like a leech.

He'd taken Rachel home that night, kissed her, breathed in the salty scent of her and believed her when she'd said she would see him in the morning. He'd floated home on a cloud of giddy, incredulous joy, thrilled that after years of hiding his feelings from her, he had done the right thing. And miraculously, she loved him, too.

It had felt as if his whole life began right then. That moment.

Those events seemed like a movie. Something he saw or read about.

He didn't recognize the kid who'd knocked on Rachel's door the morning after graduation with a cheap gold-and-cubic-zircon ring in his pocket as *him*. He didn't recognize the kid who drove to San Luis Obispo two nights later in the rain and begged her to come back with him. To talk to him. To explain to him why she was doing this.

But he recognized the man who'd driven home

that night, sick and hurt and angry. And the man who drank for two weeks straight afterward.

He knew the man who'd slept with Margaret in the middle of those two weeks and had gotten her pregnant, then done everything in his power to make his new life work.

That was him.

That was still him.

But tomorrow that was all going to change.

CHAPTER TEN

RACHEL MADE AN APPOINTMENT with Olivia for mid-morning following the Friday staff meeting. It gave Rachel enough time to fill out the paperwork DCFS loved with such a bureaucratic passion and to get a grip on the emotions that still rolled unpredictably under her feet.

She tapped her pen against the edge of her desk and stared at her wall, where she wished there was a window. She struggled to find the right words to describe the exact nature of her conflict of interest without actually saying "We were lovers and he hates me."

'Cause that wouldn't be good.

Admittedly, her late and chaotic night left her a little snarky this morning.

Finally, she settled with "We share a previously forgotten history and there is an extreme personality clash that disallows me to work on his case."

When Olivia pressed her for the full story—and she would—Rachel hoped she didn't crack like a piñata and spill the whole career-damaging tale.

She had been stupid. She realized that now, in the cold clear light of day, with Mac's hateful words resonating in her gut. It had been a disaster from the word go. The poor guy had enough on his plate without her showing up to *help*.

This was for the best. Really.

Which implied such a terrible compromise.

Rachel signed the last page of her report and stapled it into the front of Amanda's case file, on top of Frank's stuff so that the new counselor would have all of her notes, including her formal disagreement with Frank's removal assessment.

It was the best she could give Amanda.

And she hoped it was enough.

She checked her watch and decided to stop by the coffee cart and get Olivia a cookie/mood sweetener. After Rachel had begged for this case, Olivia was going to have a lot of questions and Rachel wasn't above a baked-good bribe.

She got the last oatmeal raisin cookie at the cart and had to juggle it, two coffees and the file so she could knock on Olivia's closed office door.

"Come in!" Olivia called and Rachel turned backward, pushing open the door with her butt so she wouldn't spill anything on her new mint-green tunic. Because that would be her luck today.

"Hey, Olivia, I brought you a—"

"Hey, Rachel, look who's here."

Rachel caught the sarcasm in Olivia's voice. She

turned, only to see Mac sitting in one of the chairs opposite Olivia's desk looking large and uncomfortable and so handsome things inside of Rachel constricted in response.

You didn't tell me the red-arrow case's father looks like Brad Pitt? That's what Olivia's one raised eyebrow said, and Rachel, foolish and shaken by Mac's presence, blushed. Olivia's other eyebrow hit her hairline.

"Hello, Rachel." Mac's deep voice caressed her, slid into her and took root in the soft part of her belly.

"What are you doing here?" she asked. Her jaw tightened. If he was here to make sure she got off the case...

"I was telling your boss how much we appreciate you." His blue eyes were alight with entreaty. He stood, uncurling from his chair with lean grace. He smiled at her, pure Mac charm.

The opposite of the cold-eyed man who'd torn her to shreds yesterday.

Did I dream yesterday? Am I dreaming now?

Her eyes narrowed in distrust.

"Your boss—" Mac started to say.

"Please," Olivia nearly cooed, "call me Olivia."

He smiled again and Rachel watched Olivia's one-hundred-and-eight, fully married pounds of Hispanic temper melt into her chair in response.

For the love of Pete.

"Olivia was just telling me that you are particularly good working with teenage girls and I had to agree, considering how my daughter feels about you."

Enough was enough.

"Can I speak to you outside?" Rachel asked Mac.

"Sure." Mac stepped out of the office and turned in the small hallway to wait for her.

"Leave the mood enhancer," Olivia said, and reached for the cookie and coffee Rachel had forgotten about.

"You're not breaking any rules I need to know about, are you?" Olivia whispered as Rachel bent over her desk.

"What?"

"The guy is gorgeous and you keep blushing like a schoolgirl."

"You're imagining things because you're a sucker for blondes."

"No, it's because I have a sixth sense." Olivia took the cookie and coffee.

"You have an overactive imagination." Rachel left her own coffee, but took Amanda's file and walked out to face this new incarnation of Mac.

"Rachel—" He reached out for her elbow as she passed him, but she jerked away.

"Follow me. Unless you want to cause a bigger scene in my boss's office?" she hissed.

"I'm not here to make a scene." His voice was low and contrite. "I am here to—"

"Save it for outside." Rachel was all too aware of the thin nature of cubicle walls and the gossipy nature of the men and women behind them.

She led him toward the main exit. Anger mixed with surprise built up steam in her stomach, until she was sure it escaped in white plumes from her ears.

It wasn't fair of him to show up this way. To act as if he'd never stripped her raw with his words. He'd been the one so hell-bent on reliving all of their old moments and now he showed up today as if there was nothing between them but paperwork.

She hit the push bar hard and stepped out into the dry heat of the day, her heels nearly puncturing the sidewalk. She led him to the small grassy park where this whole nightmare with the red-arrow case began.

"Rachel—"

She whirled on him. "What the hell are you doing, Mac?"

"I am here to ask you to come back."

She was baffled, stunned. "Why? You don't trust me, remember? I make you sick."

Mac blanched as the words she threw at him struck bone. "I didn't say that."

"Oh, that's right. My mistake, you said the idea of your daughter turning out like me makes you sick. Hate to get that wrong."

Mac slid his hands in the pockets of his blue jeans and smiled. "There's the Rachel I remember."

"You think this is funny?" She gave in to every strong emotion she'd tried to ignore over the past thirteen years.

"A little." He shrugged. "Obviously not funny ha-ha. More I gotta laugh or I'll start screaming."

The giant bubble of anger in her popped and she drifted, slowly but surely, back to earth.

"Why are you here?" She sighed, suddenly weary. She hugged the file to her chest as if it might protect her.

"Amanda wants you back," Mac said. "She asked me to come here and apologize."

"Really?" She couldn't help the pride that filled her. She thought she'd made a connection with the girl. It was great having that validated, but it didn't mean she'd lie down and roll over for Mac.

He nodded. "It's the first time in months that she's been insistent about something other than me leaving her alone."

"So, you're swallowing your pride for your daughter?"

"If she asked me to take off my skin, I'd do it."

Rachel collapsed onto a nearby bench. The splintering wood under her legs snagged her nylons, but she didn't care. "I'm touched, but I don't think this is going to work."

Mac sat next to her, the denim of his jeans pressed against her thigh. She could feel the heat of him through her skirt and nylons.

She crossed her legs and broke contact.

"I'm sorry for what I said. I'm sorry for the way I treated you." He turned toward her. "You coming back in my life like this was just the straw that broke the camel's back. I couldn't take all the cosmic jokes at my expense."

She smiled, but she felt more like crying. She was wrung out, all of her detachment and icy armor scattered around her like Humpty Dumpty after his great fall.

All she had left was the truth.

"I never thought about the implications my return would have on your life." She glanced at him, but couldn't look him in the eye for too long. All this emotional honesty made her feel naked. "I literally thought I'd swoop in and save the day. I am sorry I didn't think about how you would feel."

"Great, okay." He smiled. "This is progress. Will you take back the case?"

"No."

"But—"

"You were right. This is a huge conflict of interest. I could lose my job for this sort of thing." *I could lose my head, and my self-control and my independence and my sanity....*

"But Amanda needs you."

He rested his hand across the back of the bench, and though he did not touch her, she could feel the solid living heat of him.

Oh, Mac, what am I doing?

"Amanda's not going to be taken away from you, Mac. You don't have to worry about that anymore."

He tipped his head back, ran his hands through his hair and laughed. "Oh, God, what a relief."

Rachel stood, ready to end this soul-destroying goodbye scene. *How many times do I have to leave this man?* "So you don't need me, Mac. I wish you the—"

He stood, too, and his hand grabbed hers. At the touch of his flesh—calluses, muscle and bone—all the breath left her body in a loud gasp. Her nipples tightened. The hair on her arms stood up. Everything south of her navel went hot.

"She still needs you. Something is eating away at my daughter and you've been the only person in a year to reach her."

"But, Mac..." She pulled her arm free so she could think beyond the wild humming of her body. "I need you, Rachel," he whispered, and she closed her eyes against the sight of him, the sun in his hair, his heart and pride in his eyes.

I am not this strong. Not today. She couldn't handle this Mac right now. She was weak and foolhardy and wanted, more than anything, to help him. To reach out and touch his hair, his cheek rough with whiskers, his strong neck. She wanted to pull him into her arms, and be held in his.

She wanted Mac. Wanted him like she hadn't

wanted anything since the night of her high school graduation.

He laughed, the sound seemingly ripped out of him. "I never in my life thought I would be begging you again, but here I am. Rach, I'll do whatever you want. I'll play by all your rules. You're the first thing my daughter has asked me for, and I feel like if you don't come back, then I am lost. That will be it. End of story. And I'm scared, Rach. I'm scared for my daughter. I..." He looked down at his hands as if he held the answers there. "I've failed every woman I've loved. I couldn't help my mom. I couldn't help you."

Rachel went light-headed.

"I have to help my daughter—"

"Okay." The word flew out of her mouth before she could stop it. "Okay."

Mac lit up and stepped toward her as if to hug her, but she put up her hand to stop him.

"I will help your daughter."

"But...?"

No touching. Ridiculously that was what she wanted to say. *No touching. No smiling. No looking at me as if you know every secret I am hiding. No...intimacy.*

"But I can get in a lot of trouble, Mac, if Olivia finds out about our...past."

He sighed. "God, I really screwed this up. I thought if I could get you to talk about...us—" He rubbed a hand over his face. "I don't know. I thought it might help. I just wanted to get through to you. I hated how you could look at me and seem so…indifferent."

I wasn't indifferent, she wanted to say. *I was protecting myself.*

"I understand why you did that. It was stupid of me to go into your house and think that I could treat you like any other case—"

"Why do I sense a *but* coming?"

"But I am your counselor, Mac. That's all. For the sake of your family and for the sake of my job, that's all I am to you. I don't have much time to waste arguing with you. Or rehashing the past." She took a deep breath and dove headfirst into the murky waters between them. "I am so sorry for the way I treated you when we were kids."

Mac's mouth fell open.

"Between my feelings for you and my situation at home, I didn't know what to do. So I ran. I lied to you that night because I—" *Whew, this is hard.* "Because I needed you that night. But, I didn't lie when I said I loved you." There was more to it. There was the truth about how she'd felt that night when he came to her apartment in San Luis Obispo. The way her heart had answered his pleas to come back. She'd wanted to go. Wanted to forget school and the unknown cold future and go back to Mac.

But the memory of her mother, crying every time her father left, had stopped her.

"Don't leave me," Eve had begged him over and over. "I love you."

That is what love looks like. Like black eyes and empty bottles and a woman begging a man not to leave.

But Rachel wasn't about to say any of that to Mac.

Mac appeared sucker punched. He opened his mouth as if to say something and she charged ahead; these things between them needed to be put to bed so they could concentrate on what was important. Amanda.

"But I think we can both agree that things worked out for the best."

"The best?" He laughed. "From where I am standing, I think we made a mess of things."

"Mac, you have a beautiful daughter who loves you. You will get through this and see just how blessed you are. I really believe that."

Mac studied her as though she was a rock he'd turned over to find what was underneath. "What about you?" he murmured. "Where are your blessings?"

"I've got plenty." But none of them came to mind. *I've got a fish that I haven't killed yet. Sometimes I have sex with men who don't remind me of you.* "I survived my father, Mac. I got out of that house and made a life of my own. I have friends and I have a job I love. I don't want any more."

Why did that sound so sad? And so untrue.

He nodded. "I guess things really worked out for the best."

She was getting sucked into some emotional quagmire she wanted nothing to do with, so she began to make plans. "I think it's best if we could meet a few times a week." She mentally scanned her calendar. "Tuesday. I can be there by five-thirty on Tuesdays and Thursdays."

"Agreed. I think Amanda will be very happy."

"I hope so." Rachel smiled. "We'll get to the bottom of this."

He leaned in as if to hug her, and she took a hasty step back. The excited light within him diminished, faded to a respectable gray.

"Thank you, Rachel." He held out his hand and she, holding her breath, slid her palm along his. "About those things that I said. About you running and—"

"They're true. You were right." She nodded and attempted a brave smile in the face of his owlish blinking. "But I don't run out on these kids, Mac. That includes your daughter. If this is going to work, you're going to have to trust me."

He was silent.

"Can you do that?" She held her breath and waited.

"I can do that," he finally said.

He wasn't lying, but he wasn't telling the whole truth and both of them knew it. He would try.

Mac walked away and Rachel wondered if *trying* was going to save his daughter.

THREE HOURS LATER AND halfway through her progress report Rachel jumped when a manila folder landed smack-dab in the middle of her keyboard. While she typed.

"A gift." Olivia said.

"I guess interoffice mail just doesn't work for you?" Rachel scowled and deleted the line of *j*'s from the report.

"It's Christie Alvarez's file. Lois has the case and will keep it, but she said you could look at Frank's notes."

Rachel swiveled away from her computer to better face her boss, who eyed Rachel as though she was an oatmeal raisin cookie and Olivia was having a blood-sugar moment.

Beware of bosses bearing unexpected gifts.

"Thanks," Rachel said cautiously.

"Well, no problem, Rachel. No problem at all." Olivia sat down in the chair opposite Rachel's desk, crossed her legs, patted down the ruffled hem of her lemon-yellow skirt and gave her the evil eye. "Right?"

"You're asking about Mac Edwards?"

"Well, it's funny. There are quite a few things I am asking about. Yes, Mac Edwards—blond man, better-looking than a farmer should be—who, wonder of wonders, can make the unshakable Rachel Filmore blush. I am asking about the meeting you called that his visit preempted, and I am wondering why I am getting calls from a lawyer from New Springs. A Billy Martinez?"

Rachel nearly groaned.

"But I also am wondering why my friend who lectured me just a few weeks ago about detachment looks like she spent all last night crying."

Ouch. Should have taken a few more minutes with the morning makeup.

"Olivia—"

"I am asking if you have control of this case?"

Rachel straightened her shoulders and put as much steel in her voice as she could.

"I do."

"Really? Because from where I'm sitting it looks like things are heading downhill faster than you can say 'conflict of interest.'"

Rachel nodded, but Olivia's eyebrows lingered near her hairline, demanding a better answer. Rachel quickly pulled together a tangled blanket of half-truths.

"Mac Edwards was friends with my brother—"

"You have a brother?" Olivia's jaw fell open.

"We're…estranged."

"Rachel, I had no idea."

Pity, particularly in a friend's eyes, always turned knots in Rachel's stomach. "Why would you? I never told you."

"Do you want to talk about it?"

"Apparently not." She was going on approximately four minutes of sleep and a lifetime of nightmares, a combination that made her nasty. "Considering I've never talked about it before."

Olivia put up one hand. "Simmer down, Rachel. Is it a problem? This friendship of theirs?"

"Not anymore. I have made efforts to amend the relationship with my brother, and Mac and I have agreed to put that very old relationship behind us."

"Where is your brother?"

Rachel sighed. "I'm not sure." She pulled a corner of the letter she'd written last night out from under her keyboard and toyed with the edge. "But, trust me when I tell you that none of it will disrupt this case."

"What's with the New Springs lawyer?"

"Mac is a well-liked guy in town and Frank pretty much bobbled the case. Mr. Martinez is a friend looking for some answers. We have a meeting later this week."

Olivia nodded. "What about your mother?"

Rachel held up her hand. "Don't start. It's got nothing to do with—"

"I'm asking as a friend."

Rachel reined in all of the frayed ends of her life that were keeping her up nights and pulling apart her peace of mind. "I have no plan to see her." She lifted her shoulder. "Ever."

"All right, I know a brick wall when I hit my head

on it." Olivia stood and pointed her finger at Rachel. "Don't screw up."

She walked out, leaving Rachel with the distinct impression that Olivia was on to her.

CHAPTER ELEVEN

ALL IT TOOK WAS THE MERE mention of suspected sexual abuse in Lois's notes on Christie and Rachel was over the mountains and standing in front of apartment 4B in the Oakview apartment complex in New Springs.

According to Frank and Lois's file, Christie lived with her single mom. Jo Alverez worked two jobs to keep them in the "nicer" apartments across town from where Rachel had grown up.

But the dark, dank hallway Rachel stood in smelled of cat urine and marijuana. And the marijuana was coming from apartment 4B.

According to Frank, Christie behaved at a higher maturity level than Amanda, and Jo Alverez had been nothing but cooperative. Which, Rachel guessed, was why there was no red arrow on the outside of Christie's file.

Lois, on the other hand, had written concerns about Christie's oversexualized behavior.

Her grades had dipped, but had never been all

that high to begin with. But according to teachers she was a sweet girl. Helpful. Kind. Or at least she had been until about four months ago, when apparently everything went wrong. There was no question in Rachel's mind that Christie and whatever happened four months ago was the key to the fire and to Amanda's case.

Rachel stood in front of the door to apartment 4B all too aware that she wasn't supposed to be here. But Lois was out of the office and Rachel needed answers *now*.

Rachel knocked as hard as she could, but doubted she could be heard over the deafening rap music thumping behind the door. She tried again. With both fists.

"What the hell?" A girl, Rachel assumed it was Christie, wearing too much eye makeup and a shirt three sizes too small yanked open the door.

"Christie Alverez?" Rachel asked. Over the young girl's shoulder she saw two teenage boys smoking on the faded and cracked black leather couch, heads bobbing along to the music.

"Maybe." The girl sneered, cocked her hip and for all the world looked like a little girl on the road to disaster.

"I'm Rachel Filmore—"

"I heard 'bout you."

That surprised Rachel, but she kept it to herself.

"You the lady that's talking to Amanda?"

"I am. I'd like to talk to you, too."

"Hey, Christie! Shut the damn door and get back here," one of the boys yelled.

The other one poked him in the side and called out, "I'm getting cold."

"Me, too," the other one laughed, and then rubbed his crotch through his baggy jeans.

Rachel wanted to grab Christie and run.

Is this what Frank meant about maturity?

"My mom said I wasn't supposed to talk to no one unless she's around," Christie said, her eyes as old and empty as the desert this town sat on.

"What's she say about those two boys in there?" Rachel asked softly, hoping Christie would see her as the escape she clearly needed.

"My mom don't care." Christie shrugged and Rachel saw herself in that shrug. She saw every wish she'd ever made that her mother would pack her and Jesse up and get them away from their father.

"I bet you're wrong." She said it, but she didn't believe it. If Jo truly cared, this girl wouldn't be alone with two teenage boys.

"Yeah? And I bet you don't know the first thing about me and my mom."

"I'm not here to cause you trouble. I just have some questions. Talk to Amanda. She'll tell you—"

"Oh, she's told me plenty. About how you and her dad used to be together in high school and how you're back in town just to get him back—"

Rachel could not hide her shock, she nearly stumbled backward. "Amanda's wrong about that. I have a job to do and I want to help."

"Yeah, like I never heard that one before." Christie looked over her shoulder at the two boys, who stared her like starving dogs watching a piece of meat.

"Why don't you come with me now and we'll go talk to Amanda together?" It was a useless attempt, Rachel knew it, but she had to try.

"I'm busy." Christie sneered again. The look in her eyes told Rachel she knew exactly what was happening and she just didn't care. "Are you my new counselor or somethin'?"

"No—"

"Then I don't have to answer none of your questions."

The door slammed shut in Rachel's face and the music blared louder.

I should have been a chef or something. A gardener. Some job in which the failures didn't look like thirteen-year-old girls selling their bodies for a few moments of feeling wanted.

She walked away, out into the bright sunshine, which blinded after the dark hallway. She breathed in the fresh air and forced herself to think of the next thing she could do to help Amanda and, in turn, maybe Christie. Action, forward motion made most things better. Standing still never changed anything.

Christie was a dead end, so Rachel would go

back to the scene of the crime. Phone calls weren't getting her any answers, so she hoped a surprise visit would help.

GATAN MOERTE'S FARM WAS on the other side of the valley from Mac's house. As she drove she could see Mac's amazing porch and the sunlight reflecting off the sliding glass doors through the trees.

She wondered what he was doing right now. Coming in from work? Maybe he was still out in the fields, since his day had no doubt been delayed by visiting her office this morning.

Through the next break in the trees she scanned the hillside for any sign of his old blue truck.

Is he thinking about me?

The idea, stupid and irrelevant, snuck in with the rest of her thoughts about Mac and she took it as an omen to keep her mind on what she had to do today. Rather than wonder about Mac.

Running her car off the road and down the mountain would be smarter than wondering about Mac.

According to Christie's files she'd worked at the Moerte stable for a little over a year. The job paid her five dollars an hour, and six months into her tenure she'd started taking lessons on Saturdays for free. Amanda had spent time at the Moerte farm only because Christie had been there.

It didn't take a brain surgeon to see that Christie was

sexualized way beyond her years, and that was usually a product of one of two things. The early onslaught of hormonal changes—girls who got their periods in the third grade were fully developed in fifth grade and knew in their biological hardwiring what the boys were thinking when they looked at them.

The other reason little girls grew up too fast was someone helped them.

Did someone help Christie?

Rachel pulled into the wide dirt driveway in front of the Twirling G. The buildings, the fields and the fences were a beautiful study in green and white. She counted four horses watching her as they chewed grass and scratched their heads on the fence posts. The breeze smelled, ridiculously, like the climbing pink tea roses that covered the corner of the stable closest to her.

It was beautiful. A postcard.

The hair on the back of her neck went up and suspicion bit hard in her gut.

Perfection tended to hide something rotten underneath.

"Can I help you?" A middle-aged woman dressed in jeans and a faded red top stepped down from the wide porch that circled the beautiful two-story white house. She shaded her eyes with her hands and approached Rachel where she stood next to her car.

"Hi." Rachel smiled and shoved her sunglasses up on her forehead. Eye-to-eye contact went a long way with people, and she made sure to look the woman right in her brown eyes. "I'm Rachel Filmore with Santa Barbara County DCFS."

"I'm Agatha Hintches, the housekeeper." They shook hands and Rachel guessed Agatha was about fifty years old. Her red hair was turning beige at the temples, but her eyes were wide and sparkly and her handshake was as hard as a rock.

"Is Mr. Moerte around? I have a couple of questions."

Agatha shook her head. "I'm sorry, Mr. Moerte is resting. He's still recuperating from his last stroke."

"Ms. Hintches, pardon my bluntness—"

"Call me Agnes." She shrugged. "I can't ever figure out who Ms. Hintches is."

Rachel smiled. "Thank you, Agnes. I grew up around here, and—"

"Oh, I know who you are."

Rachel went still and her eyes unconsciously narrowed.

"I worked with your mom at the diner for a number of years," Agnes explained.

"Really?" The word popped out of its own accord. Rachel had never really thought of her mother having her own life, her own friends and co-workers.

"She used to tell these stories about you and your brother, Jeffery—"

"Jesse," she corrected, before she could think better of engaging in this conversation.

"Right, how could I forget? That boy." She shook her head, but her smile stayed bright. "I thought for sure he'd be the death of your mom, the way he and that Mitch Adams kicked up so much dust before they went off to the army. Anyway, she was real proud of you. Said you went off to college at CalTech."

Rachel nodded. Her throat was closed. Dry as bone.

"She always said you were the smartest one. I was sorry to have missed you all those times you came home to visit."

Rachel had to force her jaw from falling to the ground.

"Anyway." Agnes waved her hands in front of her face as if clearing the air of her chatter. "What did you want with Mr. Moerte?"

"I just wanted to ask him a few questions about the fire on his property a few months ago." Rachel asked as if in a stupor.

All of Agnes's easy smiles faded. "I'm afraid Mr. Moerte won't be able to answer those questions. Since the last stroke he's been unable to speak."

"Well, then perhaps you—"

"I already told the cops everything I know." Her easy demeanor shut down and became something uneasy. Worried. "I didn't see anything. I go home at six in the evening and I come on back at seven in the morning."

She wrung her hands once, seemed to realize

what she was doing and quickly shoved her hands in her pockets.

"Is there someone who would know more? Those two girls—"

"Are they okay?" Agnes asked, her voice a breathless gush. "I mean, the one, Christie. Is she all right?"

Rachel's blood beat hard. This woman knew something.

"No, actually she—"

"Agnes?"

Rachel and Agnes both turned to face the long, lean young man who approached them from the barn. He pushed his floppy brimmed hat off his face and smiled at the women.

Good God. He was gorgeous, tall and dark with teeth so perfect he looked like a guy in a toothpaste ad. It was as though he'd never had a mouthful of coffee.

"Hi, Jake!" Agnes shielded her face with her hand again and smiled at the man. "This here is a social worker coming to ask some questions about the fire."

"I'm Rachel Filmore." She put out her hand and he shook it, an easy handsome smile on his face.

"Jake Moerte. I'm Gatan's nephew." He shrugged affably. "We already told the police everything we know."

"So, you have no idea why those two girls would want to harm Gatan or his property?"

"Ms. Filmore, my uncle is ninety years old. He's been in a wheelchair for ten years. I have absolutely no clue why anyone, much less two kids, would single him out."

"Why didn't you press charges?" Rachel asked. Out of the corner of her eye she saw Agnes look away, a blotchy red blush building up around her neck.

Interesting.

"No one was hurt and the insurance covered the losses. I just didn't see the point in causing my uncle any more stress. Now, if it's all right, I'd like to borrow Agnes for a while. We've got some problems in the stables."

"Sure. Of course. Thanks for your help."

Jake turned away and Agnes leaned in to shake Rachel's hand.

"Say hello to your mother for me."

"I will," Rachel lied, and watched the two walk off toward the rose-covered, green-and-white stable.

"Oh." Jake turned around. "Tell Christie that we miss her around here." This time when he smiled it didn't seem so charming. It looked like the baring of teeth, the threat of violence. Agnes, beside him, didn't lift her head, she just kept walking.

That suspicion coiling in Rachel's stomach only curled tighter.

She hit the dirt road out of the Moerte farm with the hair on her neck standing at attention. Someone's eyes were on her and she would bet money that Jake watched her from the small stable windows.

Rachel's stomach growled as if she hadn't eaten

in days, and she realized it had been hours since her half of an egg salad sandwich at lunch. She decided she would go see if Mamacita's was still in business downtown. There was nothing in this world, certainly nothing in Santa Barbara, like one of Mamacita's tamales. It made her giddy just thinking about it.

She drove down the mountain and along Main Street, marveling at every block how time had passed New Springs right on by.

The sign on Price's Flowers was still missing the *P.* Half the bulbs on the movie theater marquee were burned out. Ed and Frenchy, older, but Rachel would swear they wore the same overalls, still slumped on the bench outside Moore's TrueValue.

They waved. She honked.

God, it's surreal.

Her smile faded and her stomach went cold as she passed the Main Street Café. Just the sight of the place put the taste of chocolate cream pie on her tongue, like Pavlov's dog.

The remembered cloying sweetness in the back of her throat gagged her.

But in the stagnant waters of downtown New Springs the Main Street Café flourished. She slowed her car and peered out the passenger window as she passed.

The blue-and-white storefront as well as the frame around the picture window appeared freshly painted.

The red curlicue on the *S* in *Street* was a nice touch. She remembered the paint being chipped and thin and the flower boxes being filled with cigarette butts and trash instead of cheerful red impatiens.

I was sorry to have missed you when you came back to visit.

She couldn't believe her mother had felt the need to keep up some sort of pretence of familial love. It was ludicrous, considering how they had parted.

"You'll visit, right? Christmas?" her mother had asked between drags of her cigarette. She'd sounded like a bad actress pretending to be a mother concerned about her daughter.

"No," Rachel had said, packing her meager stash of clothes into her backpack and the old duffel bag she'd borrowed from Mac. "Not if Dad's still here."

"He doesn't mean to—"

"Stop it!" Rachel had screamed. "God. Mom. Just stop it. Seventeen years of that excuse and I can't listen to it anymore! You're pathetic. You let him hurt us over and over again and we're supposed to believe that he didn't mean it?"

Her mother had just blinked, her mouth open, a string of saliva connecting her lips.

"Get out of my room," Rachel had demanded, happy to see the hurt in her mother's eyes. Delighted, actually. Thrilled in some dark and evil place in her belly.

"It's real easy for you to judge, isn't it?" Eve had said.

"Yeah, Mom, you made it real easy."

The man in the truck behind her laid on his horn and Rachel leaped, startled from that memory.

She waved, chagrined that she'd been at a complete stop in the middle of Main Street. She pulled down Second Street toward Mamacita's.

Obviously this little trip down memory lane wasn't the best idea. She'd grab a tamale and head back to the quiet safety of her apartment and her fish.

She parked outside the small Mexican restaurant that also served as a Hispanic grocery and went inside.

The gorgeous familiar smell of cumin and hot peppers seared Rachel's nose and immediately set her mouth watering. She meandered past the aisle of Hispanic soft drinks toward the back where Angelo, if he was still in charge of the restaurant, would be making her tamale dreams come true.

"Rachel?"

Rachel spun and came face to chest with Mac and Amanda, each carrying a bottle of apple soda toward one of the tables.

"What are you doing here?" Mac asked. He looked as stunned as she felt. All of Rachel's saliva dried up at the sight of him. The chill that lingered from seeing the café turned to heat and burned her from the inside.

"I wanted a tamale," she said inanely. "Hi, Amanda." She forced herself to look away from Mac's lovely and bemused eyes only to meet Amanda's level gaze.

The girl waved and a hint of a smile creased her cheek.

"Well, you can sit with us while you wait." Mac darted a quick look at Amanda as if to get permission. Amanda didn't nod, twitch or move.

"Great!" Mac said as if he'd received silent authorization. "Come sit."

Rachel followed Mac and Amanda like a lamb to slaughter to where the same four card tables that had been there when she was a teenager were surrounded by the same split and worn vinyl chairs.

What are you doing? Her better sense screamed. *Are you nuts?* This was the sort of thing that would send her already careful conflict-of-interest balancing act over the edge. Even if she didn't have a past with Mac, dinner with a family on her caseload could get her in a lot of trouble.

But, it was as though someone else pulled out the mustard-yellow chair. Someone else sat down. Someone else said yes to a basket of chips. Because there was no way. No way in the world she—Rachel Filmore—was sitting down at Mamacita's with Mac and his daughter. As if thirteen years had never passed. As if nothing had changed. As if they did this all the time.

And that was exactly why she did it. It felt too good not to.

"This place hasn't changed, has it?" Mac said, once again reading her mind.

"Aren't those the same posters?" she asked, pointing at the posters of women with huge hair and unsiliconed breasts wearing mono-kinis of all things. Pure eighties.

"I had very serious feelings for that girl when I was sixteen." Mac nodded toward a picture of a brunette with a leather jacket over her zebra-print bikini.

"Gross," Amanda whispered.

"The whole town has stayed the same. I drove down Main Street and it was like a time warp," Rachel said. She moved her elbow so a teenage girl wearing more gold jewelry than clothing could slide a plastic bowl of salsa onto the table.

"Nothing changes in New Springs—"

"But the weather." Amanda and Rachel finished Mac's old joke together, and then stared at each other, mouths agape.

"I need to get new material," Mac groused.

"If you're still using that old joke, I'd have to agree with you," Rachel said. She rolled her eyes at Amanda, ready and glad to use Mac as the common ground between them.

Amanda smiled. A real smile with shades of her father and Margaret McCormick, and suddenly sitting down with Mac and Amanda wasn't odd anymore. It wasn't threatening to her independence or peace of mind. It was right. Oddly enough, Rachel started to relax. She took the deepest breath she'd taken recently in Mac's presence and slumped in her chair, letting all the steel slide right out of her backbone.

"Have you ordered?" Mac asked, pointing at the counter and Angelo, who was working up a sweat over the ancient stove.

"No, not yet."

"I'll get it." Mac stood and approached the counter.

Rachel leaned toward Amanda. "Does he still do that thing when he orders tamales?"

"He's added to it." Amanda rolled her eyes and Rachel groaned.

"I can't watch." Rachel clapped a hand over her eyes. Her heart tripped and lifted into her throat when Amanda giggled.

"Can I have…" Mac said in what might be the worst Spanish accent ever attempted by a white man. Rachel moved her hand, suddenly dying to see the old gag. "Four hot tamales!" He put goofball emphasis on *hot* and waved his hands as if his fingers were burning. "And I mean hot!"

"Chicken or beef?" Angelo asked. The big man was clearly not amused, but Rachel could not stop laughing. Even Amanda smiled.

"Chicken." Mac turned and pointed at her. "Still chicken, right?"

"Still chicken," Rachel said, past a painful lump in her throat.

"You and Dad used to come here?" Rachel turned to see Amanda studying her.

"All the time." Rachel swallowed but the jagged chunk of emotion stayed persistently lodged in her throat. "Angelo used to let us come in at night after he closed."

"Why didn't you go home?" Amanda asked. "Because of your dad?"

Sitting in this stew of memories with Mac hamming it up at the counter, she didn't feel like lying or hedging.

"Mostly because of *your* dad."

"Did you love him?"

A vacuum opened up in Rachel and sucked out every rational response. All she could do was blink. And stare.

"I found all his stuff from high school. I think he loved you." Amanda fiddled with the string of her blue hooded sweatshirt and Rachel felt the knife buried in her heart twist.

Before Rachel could get her lungs working or even get her jaw up off the floor Mac was back with the corn-husk-wrapped delicacies.

"Four hot tamales, for two hot tamales."

"Dad," Amanda groaned, like a normal twelve-year-old.

"I know, I know, new material." He smiled at Rachel, but some of her distress must have shown on her face because his smile faded. "Rach? You okay?"

"She's just hungry," Amanda said, filling the silence Rachel was too stunned to fill on her own. "Right?" Her blue eyes bored into Rachel's with a million unasked questions. A million secrets. And a sort of understanding. A knowledge that Rachel thought for a split second was meant for her.

I know what you want, Amanda's eyes seemed to say. *I know all about you.*

"Starved." Rachel reached for one of the baskets on Mac's tray. "Well, I better get going...."

"Have a safe—"

"Stay," Amanda said, and this time Mac's mouth fell open. "Tamales are hard to eat in the car."

Rachel and Mac stared at each other, and she could only guess that he was making the same calculations she was, the same careful adding and subtracting of dangers and risks and longings and nostalgia. She wanted to stay, but it would cost her, and at this point she didn't know what she had left to give.

He shrugged minutely. "She's right, you'll be a mess by the time you get home."

Rachel saw no way out that wouldn't reveal her as a coward, so she committed herself to this lunacy.

"Okay." She smiled at Amanda, who tentatively smiled back. "I'll just go grab a soda."

Rachel stood and made her way to the cooler in the store part of the building, hoping some refrigeration would cool her down.

As soon as Rachel was out of earshot Mac spun to face his daughter. She peeled open the corn husk around her tamale as if performing open-heart surgery.

"What has gotten into you?"

"What?" she asked, waving the steam away.

"You want to have dinner with Rachel? Your counselor?" *I must be dreaming.* Mac looked in the corners for his fifth-grade teacher or a giant rabbit or some other sign that this was a nighttime vision. But no rabbits. Just the very real smell of Mexican food and his daughter, who was about as readable as Arabic.

"Don't you?" Amanda asked.

"Don't I what?" Mac lost focus. Rachel approached them carrying a lime soda, which he'd known she would pick because that was all she ever drank in high school, and the knowledge—the way that he *still* knew her—blew his mind.

"Don't you want to have dinner with Rachel?" Amanda asked. "You're staring at her, Dad."

"What?" Mac jerked his head back to his daughter. *I am. I am staring at Rachel. My daughter is eating and I am losing my mind. Perfect.*

"Everything okay?" Rachel asked, sitting down as if the past thirteen years had never happened.

"Peachy!" Mac shoveled a bite of cornmeal and chicken into his mouth and scorched his tongue.

Just peachy.

AMANDA CAUGHT THE LIME SODA bottle before it crashed onto the floor. She set it down carefully next to the two beer bottles Dad nearly knocked over a few minutes ago when he laughed so hard beer came out his nose.

"Mac, stop it!" Rachel shrieked. She slapped the table again, which was how the first bottle had nearly crashed. "You are lying to your daughter. I never ran after Joe Gilbert and I *never* dyed my hair purple."

Dad and Rachel acted the way she and Christie used to when they ate too many gummy bears.

It was hilarious. Weird. But hilarious.

"It's the truth! Amanda?" Her dad turned to her and held out his hand. "Do you believe me?"

"No," Amanda said, and her father groaned.

"Thank you." Rachel nodded at her as though she was the queen. "At least someone in your family has good sense."

"Traitor," Dad muttered, and Amanda bit the insides of her cheeks so that her smile wouldn't split her whole face apart.

She had never—ever—seen her father this happy, and it made her chest hurt, as though something was smashing her.

"I don't have to remind you of the time your toga fell off during the homecoming pep rally." Rachel folded her napkin into little squares, but she watched Dad out of the corner of her eyes.

They are totally into each other.

"Nope, no reminder necessary."

"Why were you wearing a toga to a pep rally?" Amanda asked. God, he really was a dork.

"Yeah, Mac. Why were you wearing that toga—"

"Well, I can't believe my eyes!"

Crap!

Everybody turned to face Mr. Martinez, who stood behind Dad holding a bag of tamales.

"Hey, Billy!" Dad reached out to shake Mr. Martinez's hands, and Amanda watched all the fun bleed right out of Rachel until she turned back into the pale, uptight woman she'd been when she walked in.

Double crap.

"Billy Martinez, this is…" Dad paused for a second and faked a little half cough.

Uh-oh.

"Rachel Filmore," Rachel filled in, standing up from her chair to shake Mr. Martinez's hand. "We talked last week."

"Rachel Filmore, the counselor? From DCFS?" Mr. Martinez didn't look too happy about that, and Dad looked as if he'd eaten a whole spoonful of the green salsa. Amanda wondered if they were breaking rules. Well, obviously they were breaking rules, but Amanda just didn't understand which ones. Or why. It would be stupid for there to be a rule that said Dad and Rachel couldn't have tamales or tell stories or that Dad, for the first time in as long as Amanda could remember, couldn't laugh his big, loud laugh that she had missed so much.

Those were stupid rules.

"The same." Rachel was as cool as water. "I hope we're still on for our meeting tomorrow."

"Yes." Mr. Martinez totally went into lawyer mode. "I'm looking forward to it. I have some questions."

"Great, I do as well." Rachel smiled, but it was sharp like a knife. She stood up and swung her purse over her shoulder and grabbed her red plastic food basket to take up to the counter.

"Mac, Amanda, thank you for inviting me to dinner." She smiled, but it was as if she was saying goodbye to people trying to sell her something, instead of the people who had just a few minutes ago, had her laughing so hard she'd cried.

Amanda wanted to scream. The quiet sliced at her, the way it used to when Mom was alive. All the things that Rachel and Dad and Mr. Martinez wanted to say, but didn't think they should, filled the air with razor blades so that it hurt to breathe.

Just say it! she wanted to shout.

Of course last time she'd said that to her mom, Mom had ended up dead. So maybe Amanda would just keep her mouth shut.

"Goodbye, Rachel." Dad's voice held the same quiet rasp Amanda had grown so used to she'd forgotten he had another voice. A happy one.

"Good night." Rachel smiled and nodded at everyone the same amount before she left, as if making a point of not showing favorites. Her pretty brown curls glowed red, then blue as she walked under the neon lights.

"Jesus, Mac," Mr. Martinez muttered through a tight jaw. "What the hell are you doing?"

"It's fine, Billy. We're fine." Dad started wadding up their used napkins and throwing them in the baskets.

Things weren't fine. And everybody knew it, but Dad, Rachel and even Mr. Martinez were all pretending that it was some kind of secret they had to keep to protect her.

God. If they only knew the secrets she held to keep all of them safe.

CHAPTER TWELVE

RACHEL PUSHED OPEN HER office door the next morning only to find Olivia sitting at her desk.

"Good morning," Rachel said. "You want to switch offices?" She hung up her jacket, pretending that Olivia sitting in the dark in Rachel's office before work was all normal. But it wasn't, and Rachel guessed that sinking feeling in her stomach might just be the bottom dropping out of her career.

"I want you to drop the Edwards case." Olivia didn't waste any time. She circled the desk and stood in front of her. "Today. This minute."

"I—I can't." Rachel shook her head and wished she didn't sound so desperate.

"I don't care if you can or can't. You will. Billy Martinez called me this morning—"

"Oh, for crying out loud," she muttered, and dropped her bag on the chair beside her. "What a tattletale."

"Do you think this is funny?" Olivia's temper leaped to life in her eyes.

"No, I think it's being blown out of proportion."

"Oh, really? Which part? The part that has you eating dinner with a family in your caseload?"

"Yes, actually." Olivia's sarcasm had Rachel worried. Her boss was mad, madder than Rachel had ever seen her. "That part. We just ran into each other."

"Sure, I can understand that."

"Then what's the big deal?"

"The big deal is you lied." Olivia jabbed a rigid finger at her. "You said Mac Edwards had a relationship with your brother. You never breathed a word about the relationship you had with him. Billy Martinez did some asking around about you."

"What—"

"Do not take me for a fool!" Olivia shouted.

Damn Billy Martinez.

"Okay." Rachel held out her hands as if Olivia was holding a gun to her career. Which she was. Rachel swallowed and tried to talk the whole situation down from the ledge. "We were friends growing up."

"Mr. Martinez tells me it's a well-known fact that there was something more between you than friendship."

Damn small-town gossip.

"There was. Once—"

"You're off the case. You're on probation."

"Olivia!"

"You're lucky we're friends. Frank would have had your resignation on his desk by the end of the day."

"I can't leave Amanda now. I can't. We're so close."

"And you're close to throwing away six years with this department. You are way past code red, Rachel. I've been warning you for weeks to stay on top of this case. What's happened to you?"

Mac's happened to me. Amanda's happened to me. I sat around a table and laughed last night. Harder than I have in years. That's what's happened. I feel good. I feel...happy.

"Give me one more day. One more day and then I'll drop it. You can demote me."

"I am not going to argue with you, Rachel. You resign the case or you leave the department. It's your call."

She could resign but stay involved. Unofficially and below Olivia's radar. There was no way Rachel would leave Amanda now. There was no way she could leave Mac now. Not again. There was too much riding on the next few days. Not just Mac, not just Amanda, but something was in this for her, too.

"Fine. I resign."

Olivia shook her head. "Do you think I'm stupid?"

"No—"

"If I hear one word of you even driving over those mountains, it will be your job. One word to the Edwards girl and you will be fired. So, don't think you can fool me by resigning but still keeping your hand in this case."

Her back was against the wall and she didn't even have to think about it. She didn't even pause. Something was happening to her, some change in her cells and blood. Her molecules were reorganizing and she wasn't entirely sure who she was anymore, but she felt better for the changes. She felt as though, for the first time in her life, she could see herself clearly. And it was because she'd dropped the detachment. She'd helped Amanda, and if she walked away from her now, what would happen? The thought of Mac's nightmare stretching on when Rachel had the power to end it twisted her stomach. She couldn't do it.

She'd seen her own reflection in Mac's eyes, in his face and his family. She'd made a difference for him, she'd changed him and been changed, and she couldn't go back on that now. What would it say about her if once more she chose herself over people who needed her? She'd done that before and it had been a disaster. If she did it again, it would destroy her. She knew that as well as she knew anything.

"You'll have my resignation at the end of the day."

Olivia blinked. "Are you serious?"

Rachel nodded.

"You're throwing your career away for an old boyfriend?"

"He's more than an old boyfriend, Olivia. He's a friend and the best man I've ever known. He deserves my help. Amanda deserves my help. They need me."

"I hope he's worth it," Olivia muttered, and

walked out. The door slammed behind her, the shades banging against the window.

"He is," Rachel breathed, and hoped she could pull herself, Mac and Amanda away from the suction of her sinking career.

BE COOL, Mac told himself. *Just resist every impulse you've got and be cool.*

The doorbell rang and immediately he was drenched in nervous sweat.

"That's cool, Mac. Real cool," he muttered as he took the steps two at a time to the front door.

He mopped his forehead and opened the door, hoping the smile on his face was a cool, slick, dev-il-may-care grin, rather than an I-had-an-X-rated-sex-dream-about-you-last-night leer.

"Hi, Mac," Rachel said, as calm as the blue California sky behind her. She wore a green blouse that made her eyes gleam like gold coins. "I hope it wasn't too much trouble meeting earlier."

"No problem." Thank God, his voice didn't crack. The problem was the dream he'd had last night following their surprise dinner at Mamacita's. In it, he'd seen *a lot* more of Rachel and he'd woken up turned-on, alone and feeling foolish. That dream lay like a veil over both of them, and he couldn't look at her without thinking about the things he'd dreamed she'd done to him.

Mac stepped aside and Rachel walked in.

"Amanda, Rachel's here," he yelled toward the stairs, realizing too late that he had shouted in Rachel's ear.

"Sorry," he muttered.

"It's okay, Mac. I'm a little freaked-out, too." Her lips curled and she shot him a saucy and sympathetic look from the corner of her eye that was pure Rachel, and it made all of his stupidity okay.

"How'd it go with Billy?" Mac shut the door behind Rachel and gestured for her to go on down to the kitchen.

She shrugged. "Fine."

"He didn't give you the third degree?"

"Well, I think I convinced him that I don't want to kill you and Amanda and bury you in my backyard, but I wouldn't say I convinced him of anything else. That is one suspicious guard dog you've got there."

"I'm sorry." Mac winced. "He's been a good friend for the past year. He and his wife think of us as part of—"

"Oh, that's very clear." Rachel laughed and slid her briefcase onto the island that just seconds ago he'd wiped clean of the breakfast crumbs and spilled grape jelly. "You are Billy Martinez's family." Rachel's smile was soft and sweet and pulled on all of his nerve endings. "I think it's wonderful, Mac, that you have friends that feel that way about you and Amanda. You always were a good friend. You deserve to be treated the way you treat people." She busied herself with her files, as if looking for something of great importance at the bottom of her bag.

She seemed to imply that he deserved more than what she'd given him. And he really couldn't stand that she thought that. They'd had four years of friendship before graduation night ruined it all.

"You were a good friend to me," he said. "The best I'd ever had. You just weren't a very good girlfriend."

Rachel smiled but continued to look for something in her bag. "Thanks, Mac. That's good to hear."

She clutched her bag as if she might drown without it, and he knew the feeling. He could barely stay afloat in the dark waters between them. Every moment they spent together without trying to hurt each other made the water rise.

"Rachel." He lifted a hand to touch her bone-white knuckles. "I had fun last night."

A blush climbed her pale neck. "So did I," she murmured. "I haven't had a good time like that in years."

Her honesty rocked him and mimicked his own thoughts. Was it possible she felt the same pull of the past? The same painful grip of nostalgia and missed opportunities? His fingers grazed her fist, the satin of her skin, the slight clammy sweat that excused his own drenching.

I want to do it again. He was a breath away from saying it. *I want to see you again, like that. Laughing and happy. I missed that. I missed you.*

"Hi," Amanda said from the landing, and Mac jerked his hand back.

"Hi, sweetie." He was too loud. Too jovial. Too "caught touching the counselor" and he could tell Amanda knew it. "Come on down, I'll just leave you two alone."

"Aren't we going to go for a walk?" Amanda asked.

Rachel blinked. "You want to walk?"

Amanda shrugged.

"That's a yes in my daughter's shrugging language," Mac translated.

"Then we'll walk." Rachel left her briefcase and joined Amanda at the landing. She pulled open the door and the sunlight streamed in through the screen. Rachel and Amanda were framed by the yellow pine that he'd finished himself and the bright blue sky behind them. The sun gilded Amanda's hair and turned Rachel's skin to gold.

They're all I've ever wanted, he thought, breathless and sad.

"Bye, Dad." Amanda waved.

"Bye, Mac," Rachel said, mimicking Amanda's wave and girlish singsong voice that was so rare and so beautiful.

"Bye, girls." He made every effort to be jolly. To be smiley and happy and easygoing, but when the door shut behind them Mac collapsed into a chair and held his head in his hands.

With all the distrust and anger gone, his heart

seemed hell-bent on reminding him that Rachel
Filmore was the only girl he'd ever loved.

Get a grip, man. He forced himself to stand up.
To go on with his day. *She didn't stay thirteen years
ago and it's not like she's going to stay now.*

And worse, he wasn't sure he wanted her to stay,
despite his heart's wild impulses. He didn't think he
was strong enough.

RACHEL WAS NOT SURE from what angle Amanda
would strike. Her foundation was shaken. She'd
given up her job. Defended her honor to Billy
Martinez, who clearly thought she was out to feed
Mac and Amanda to the dogs, and now she was
bending state law by talking to Amanda.

All in all it was a heck of a day for a woman
who prided herself on detachment. She was so
detached she'd nearly thrown herself into Mac's
arms a few minutes ago. A couple more seconds
alone with him and she'd have done it. The effects
of last night still lingered in her blood like wine.
The laughter and the sense of belonging had gone
to her head and filled her dreams and…well, cost
her her job.

All that for two lime sodas and a tamale.

But she didn't regret it. Not for a minute. She
glanced at Amanda. Her thin shoulders barely filled
out her pink sweatshirt. Her stick-figure legs hardly
seemed capable of carrying her weight. A change in

counselors right now would send this wounded but smart girl into a tailspin.

Rachel hoped Mac never knew what this decision cost her. It was partly her pride—being fired didn't sit well with her. But she didn't have answers for the questions he'd have if he found out that she'd chosen him and Amanda over her all-important career.

Here I am, she thought, *without that job and I'm still breathing.* In fact, she was breathing better than ever.

She just couldn't tell Mac that. Not yet.

She braced herself for Amanda's questions about Mac or maybe even about Billy.

"I know who your mom is," Amanda said as they stepped onto the road.

Rachel reeled. *Was not expecting that one.*

"Is that important to you?" she finally managed to ask. "To know who my mom is?"

Amanda shot her a "no-duh" look. "Isn't it important to you to know who *my* mom was?"

Jesus, this girl is too smart for her own good.

Rachel nodded and kicked at a stone. "I think it's important for you to talk about your mom."

Amanda pursed her lips and remained silent.

"Do you miss your mom?" More silence.

This girl is too stubborn for her own good.

"Do you miss yours?" Amanda asked. "Since you never come back here you must not see her much."

Rachel swallowed. She knew the second she said,

"We're not talking about that," Amanda would clam up. The key to effective counseling was to make the parameters of the conversation invisible. Give a little and then steer a little, all so the client didn't know. "Sometimes," she said. "I met Christie yesterday—"

"Was your mom mean?" Amanda asked.

Rachel sighed inwardly and nodded. "Sometimes. Was yours?"

Amanda laughed through her nose. "You could say that."

"Was she mean to you?"

"Not as mean as she was to my dad."

Rachel forced herself not to react, but her heart cried for Mac. "What's Christie's mom like?" Rachel asked. "She wasn't there when I stopped by after school."

"She works a lot." Amanda shrugged.

"Is that why Christie got the job at the stables?" Rachel asked. "So she'd have something to do after school?"

Amanda picked up a small black rock from the road and bounced it in her palm.

"When you said your mom was mean to you, what were you talking about? Like, did she yell at you?" Amanda wasn't going to let go of Rachel's mother.

"Well…" Rachel searched for some kid-friendly way to say "she was a cowardly bitch." "She never stopped my dad when he hurt my brother and me. And she never got us away from him. You know, Christie wasn't alone when I—"

"My mom used to be real nice," Amanda said, clearly uninterested in talking about Christie. "She was, like, the prettiest mom out of all my friends."

"Then what happened?"

"I don't know." Amanda shrugged. "She just started yelling at my dad all the time, and when he wouldn't yell back she'd leave. Once she left for a week."

"Were you scared? When she left."

Amanda nodded. "But then she came back and things were worse. Dad said we have to forgive people, but I couldn't."

"That's a hard thing to do."

"Have you forgiven your mom?"

Rachel nearly laughed. "No. I haven't."

"Dad says sometimes people do things that hurt other people without knowing it. They do it because they're hurting, too."

"Your dad is a smart guy." She wondered if Mac gleaned that knowledge from what she'd done to him.

"Do you ever wish she was dead?" Amanda's voice was small, and Rachel stopped walking to stare at her. "Your mom," she clarified.

"I used to. Amanda, do you want to tell me something about how your mom died?"

"It was a car accident."

"I know, but since you were in the car, maybe there's something you want to tell me."

"I was asleep."

"Okay." She'd seen this a million times before.

Kids and parents get into fights and one of them tells the other that they wished the other was dead. There's a terrible accident and someone is left with a burden of guilt so large the rest of their lives get crushed by it. "But you know wishing your mother was dead doesn't kill her. It takes more than wishes to make a car hit a tree."

Amanda stopped walking and stared down at her feet.

"Is there something you want to talk about? Maybe if you tell me you'll feel better," Rachel breathed. *Please tell me. Please tell me.*

Amanda looked up and her eyes were dry but blazing. "I followed your mom home from work the other day."

"Amanda—" Rachel was ready to put an end to this little who-had-the-worst-mom game Amanda seemed so hell-bent on playing.

"You grew up in a real shit hole." Amanda's face twisted into something old and ugly. "Your mom doesn't look too good, either. I bet she's sick or something."

The words punched Rachel. Branded her. Sunk into her soft tissue and took chunks out of her living flesh. She had to force herself to breathe and to stay rooted to the ground. She wanted to turn and run as far away from this girl and her hurtful words as possible.

"I don't think you really want to talk about my

mother." She sounded like a woman without air, but it was the best she could do.

"Well, I don't want to talk about mine anymore."

"Then let's talk about Christie."

Amanda scowled at Rachel as though she were scum.

"She wasn't by herself when I stopped by after school. She was with two older boys."

"She's always got boys around her these days."

"Was she always like that?"

"No." Amanda sneered. "She used to be normal and come over to my house every day after school."

"She doesn't do that stuff anymore?"

"I don't want to talk about this shit."

"Then what do you want to talk about?"

"Why didn't you and my dad get married?"

Rachel had to take a step back or fall over. "Amanda, that's none—"

"None of my business?" Amanda's cheeks burned. "You have no clue what my business is."

"Are Christie and those boys your business?"

"Of course. I keep all the secrets, Rachel. I know about you and Dad and Christie and the boys—"

Rachel took a risky stab in the dark, driven by her own hurt and frustration. "What about Jake Moerte? Is he your business?"

Amanda turned white. Her lips trembled.

Jackpot.

"What do you know about Jake?" she whispered.

"I met him yesterday and he asked about Christie."

Amanda's mouth fell open and tears magnified the anger and rage in her bright blue eyes.

"What'd he say?"

"Amanda—"

"What did he say about Christie?"

"He said he missed her."

Amanda crumpled. Right in front of Rachel's eyes, she fell in on herself. Her face collapsed into a mask of grief and confusion that was so painful to see, tears blurred Rachel's vision.

Rachel took a slow, careful step toward her. "If he's got something to do with what happened—"

"Is he going to hurt Christie?" Amanda whispered, the pain in her voice scratching Rachel's heart.

"Has he hurt her before?"

"Can he hurt her?" Amanda screamed.

"Yes." Rachel nodded. "He can, unless you know something that might—"

"It's supposed to be a secret," Amanda cried. "Christie said it was a secret. I promised. I promised." Amanda sobbed and Rachel put a tentative hand on the girl's shaking shoulders.

"Amanda, you can tell me. If Jake did something bad to Christie, he should be punished. And if you know something and tell me, then you are helping Christie, not hurting her. Keeping this a secret is hurting both of you."

"I just can't keep all these secrets anymore!" The girl sobbed and Rachel curled her hand over Amanda's small shoulder and pulled her close.

"You don't have to. You don't have to," Rachel murmured into Amanda's cornstalk hair.

Amanda clutched Rachel, her knees giving way under her meager weight. Rachel wrapped her arms around her to keep them both upright.

"Amanda," Rachel urged, "did Jake hurt Christie? Is that why you guys started the fire?"

Amanda's nod was nearly imperceptible, but Rachel felt it against her shoulder. Her heart spasmed and relief made her fingers and toes go numb. Her own knees nearly buckled.

"What did he do, Amanda?" She already knew, in the pit of her sour stomach, what that bastard had done. But Amanda needed to get these demons out, or they'd eat her alive.

"He used to come in when she was cleaning the stables—" She stopped, shook her head against Rachel's shoulder.

"It's okay, take your time."

Slowly, Amanda got the whole story out. Christie had been working at the stables for about two months when Jake started paying special attention to her.

"She used to think he was so nice, the way he always hung around her and talked to her about her mom." Amanda wiped her eyes with the heel of her hands.

But the special attention turned to inappropriate

comments, which became touching and then finally Jake raped Christie in the stables.

"Christie was so mad. She said she was going to go burn down the farm. She wanted to get back at Jake."

"Why didn't she go to the police?"

Amanda gave her an adult look that knew too much about shame and distrust. A look that told her that was a stupid question, and it was. Rachel smiled sadly in the face of Amanda's forced maturity.

"Why did you go with her?" Rachel asked.

"I couldn't let her go alone. I thought I could talk her out of it, but then…" Amanda held herself so still, so brittle that Rachel worried the slightest touch would break her into a million pieces. "I just didn't want her to get hurt."

"Of course you didn't. Sh. Sh." Rachel rocked Amanda in her arms when she began sobbing in huge shudders again. She pressed kisses to her hair and whispered in her ear all of the calming things she could think to say, and after a while, Amanda's shaking faded to a persistent tremble.

"You are a strong girl, Amanda. So brave," Rachel whispered fiercely.

"Do we have to tell my dad?"

"I think we should, don't you?"

Amanda nodded. "What happens now?"

"Well, you talk to your dad and I am going to call the police."

"Is Christie going to be arrested?"

"No. But you will need to go talk to the police."

"Will you come with me?"

Rachel had a tough time breathing for a moment, strangled by relief and gratitude. "Of course," she finally whispered. "Of course I will."

MAC GAVE A PRETTY GOOD rendition of casual dad, just working in the garage, but he didn't fool Rachel. He stood in the doorway of the garage, far away from any tool or piece of equipment with a rag in his hand. As soon as he caught sight of her holding Amanda against her side as they walked back to the house, he dropped the rag and ran out onto the gravel road to meet them.

Usually these moments between parents and kids, after a breakthrough, were moments of extreme pride for Rachel. She accepted the thanks and praise with humility and gratitude that it had all worked out. These were the moments she worked toward, these sweet reunion scenes with tears and hugs. These were the rewards for her hard work.

But the tears in Mac's eyes destroyed her pride and she was no longer the kind benefactor, the enabler of this scene, she was in it. Living it. Wallowing knee-deep in the messy and painful emotions that filled the yard.

"Amanda! What happened? Are you okay?" He cupped his daughter's splotchy, tear-streaked face with tender, trembling hands.

She couldn't breathe. Her heart ached. The facade of counselor crumbled around her like dust, and she was left with all her human nerves and longings exposed to the bitter winds. Rachel had to look away, blinded by tears and the sharp agony of feeling way too much.

"Sweetheart?" he said. "Are you okay? What…?"

Rachel untangled herself from Amanda. *I have to go. I have to leave. I've done my job. It's time to go.*

Amanda let go of her and clung to her father like a vine, but Rachel could still feel Amanda shaking. She felt it in her gut, in her chest, under her heart. A fine quiver like glass about to break.

Rachel pressed shaky hands to shaky lips.

"Daddy, I am sorry. I am so sorry," Amanda wailed into his chest. Mac's eyes over his daughter's head were filled with confusion.

"What's going on?" he asked.

"Amanda has something to tell you," Rachel managed to say. "It looks like everything's going to be okay."

Rachel focused on Amanda's hair so she wouldn't see the searing, heart-stopping combination of wonder and joy that suffused his face and made her long for the right to witness this moment. To be a part of it. To be sheltered in the long strong arms of Mac Edwards.

But she didn't have that right. She'd thrown it away without knowing how much it was worth.

"Sh," Mac whispered into his daughter's hair. "Sweetheart, it's okay. It will be okay."

Rachel walked into the house because her heart could no longer take the proof that Mac's life—his home, family and the love that he handed out so easily—was priceless. And completely beyond her reach.

AFTER CALLING THE POLICE, Rachel left a message on Olivia's phone. The police would be contacting Christie and her mother and, after that, hopefully picking up Jake on charges. Rachel left another message for Lois, Christie's caseworker, telling her the same thing and giving her Agatha Hintches's name. The woman knew more than she was saying.

Rachel's job was done. Literally.

She hung up and grabbed her bags. She would drive her own car to the station and then leave from there. She didn't need to come back to Mac's house again. The bite of tears returned.

What an idiot, she chastised herself, but it did little to help. She felt so close to the edge of that emotional cliff that she'd spent the past thirteen years trying to get away from. When she'd walked away from Mac, she'd walked away from strong emotions, the push and pull of want and denial. And now, here she was in Mac's kitchen, staring those emotions in the face.

And she longed to avoid it all, to walk away from everything she wanted.

Mac and Amanda stepped into the house.

"I guess we have to go to the police station?" Mac asked, his arm wrapped around Amanda as though he'd never let go.

"Amanda needs to file a report." Rachel nodded and swung her bag over her shoulder.

"Where are you going?" Amanda asked, lifting her head from her father's side.

"I can meet you at the station—"

Amanda shook her head. "You said you'd stay."

"Amanda." Mac jumped in ready to let her off the hook, ready to give Rachel the out, the chance to fall back on her old tried-and-true behavior. "Rachel is very busy, she might—"

"You said you would come!" Amanda's voice was a gasping plea.

"Of course, of course. I'll leave my car here," Rachel said quickly, to stem the flare of hysteria that she and Amanda were both clearly feeling.

Rachel walked across the kitchen toward the edge of that cliff with her head up and her shoulders back. She couldn't run. Not now. She gazed at Mac's worn and tired face, more cherished for the hard miles on it, and knew she'd been lying to herself for a while.

She'd been a goner the second she'd stepped back into Mac's life.

CHAPTER THIRTEEN

Two EMOTIONALLY EXHAUSTING hours later, Mac carefully juggled his sleeping daughter in his arms so he could pull his house keys out of his front pocket.

"Here—" Amanda slipped and the keys fell back into his pocket. "Sorry. I can't—"

Without looking at him Rachel slid her hand into his front pocket. She was in and out before he could register the heat and touch of her through the worn cotton of his jeans.

"Got it," she breathed. She turned and dealt with the lock. Mac watched the moths buzz around the light over his front door, and he hugged his fragile daughter to his chest.

Everything happens for a reason. Cindy, his wise mother-in-law, always said that sort of thing when it felt as if the whole world was falling in around him. He could honestly say he'd never really wondered about the truth of that statement before this moment.

Amanda sighed and turned her face into his armpit.

What series of events, what cosmic plan brought Rachel back to him just in time to save his family?

Finally Rachel got the door open and she eased inside the dark house.

"Wait for me," he whispered. She hadn't looked him in the eyes once since she and Amanda had returned from their miraculous walk, which was fine. He was one step away from spinning apart—splintering out into the heavens—and one look from her, one sympathetic, kind, warm glance from her familiar eyes and he'd be on his knees in tears.

She nodded and he carried his daughter up the stairs. He nudged open the door with his foot and carefully picked his away through the minefield of dirty clothes and books and CDs to lay Amanda down on her bed.

His vision clouded with tears. His breath hitched in his throat.

Thank you. Thank you. Thank you.

He brushed the hair from Amanda's small face and slipped the yellow flip-flops off her feet. He cradled her foot in his hand, touched the remains of the glittery pink toenail polish she wore. She twitched and sighed, rolled to her side and her foot slid from his hand.

He fell to his knees beside the bed, no longer able to stand. Barely able to breathe. He wiped his mouth with trembling hands and tried not to sob like a baby. Tried to control his relief and gratitude so his daughter would not wake up.

Thank you, God, for bringing Rachel back into my life.

After a long moment, listening to the quiet rasp of his daughter's breathing and counting his suddenly overwhelming blessings, he finally stood and left Amanda sleeping in the slight pool of moon and star light that filtered in through her eyelet curtains.

He touched the ladybugs on the light-switch plate as he passed and wondered what would happen in the morning. What creature would emerge from this room?

He shut the door and decided tomorrow morning would take care of itself. Tonight, on the other hand, he had plans.

Mac could barely see Rachel in the shadows of the unlit kitchen. Moonlight streamed in through the sliding glass door, making a map of light and dark territories out of his kitchen.

"Can I turn on the light?" he asked.

"Of course. I would have but I couldn't find the switch." Her husky voice floated through the intimate, warm darkness and wrapped around him. Filled his head like whiskey with thoughts about a friendship that had always felt like more. About being lonely and wanting to celebrate the return of normalcy with something…wicked.

"Let's go out on the patio," he suggested, his voice a heavy hum in the air between them.

"All right." She stood, and he could feel the vibrations in the air. He could hear the sound of her clothes shifting and moving over her body.

"You want a beer?"

"Sure."

He grabbed the beers from the fridge and led the way outside, aware of her heat and her smell behind him.

On the patio the breeze blowing through the valley cooled him momentarily. But then Rachel stood beside him at the railing and her shoulder grazed his, her hips bumped his, then shifted away. That dance—that awareness—blazed between them like a bonfire. He melted like metal under a blowtorch. He lost all sense of himself in the heat. He worried the love-starved teenager in him would try to make this night into something more. A new beginning. A second chance.

Because it wasn't. Tomorrow was about Amanda and getting his family back on solid ground.

Tonight was about goodbye. And thanks. And a young love that had never stood a chance.

"Long night," Rachel murmured, taking one of the bottles from his hand.

"I'll say."

"She was so brave in the interview room." Rachel shook her head. The moonlight turned her cheeks to pearl. "I've never seen a kid keep it together like that."

"Thank you—"

She held up her hand. "Don't."

"I know it's your job, but I can't thank you enough."

She laughed, but the sound wasn't happy.

"So, I guess there will be a bunch of paperwork to fill out, right? Will we have to go back to court?"

"I'm not sure. It depends." Rachel took a big swig of beer and averted her face to look up at the night sky.

"Depends on what?" he asked, wary of whatever she seemed to be hiding.

She heaved a huge sigh. "It depends on your new counselor."

"You're quitting?" Fireworks went off in his brain. "You're leaving us now? Running again?"

"Actually, Mac, I was fired for *not* leaving you."

"Fired?" He went numb with shock.

"Well, forced to resign."

"You better start from the beginning, Rachel. I'm lost. You lost your job because of Amanda and me?"

"Actually, I think I lost my job because your friend Billy's got a protective streak a mile wide. After I called him, he did some checking and found out we went to high school together. He must have asked around and gotten suspicious. He's called Olivia before, but I don't think he discussed our prior relationship. But after he saw us together at Mamacita's he called my boss and told her." Rachel rolled the bottle between her hands. "Olivia told me to give up the case or give up my job." She smiled, but it didn't reach her eyes. "I chose you."

I chose you.

The words sent off rockets and avalanches in his body. God, if only she'd done that thirteen years ago, they wouldn't be in this mess.

He knew better than to feel guilty for a decision *she'd* made, but still guilt settled around his shoulders like a hair shirt. "I'll call Billy and have him talk to Olivia—"

Rachel shook her head. "Don't bother. I need a little time off. I've got some things I need to figure out."

Am I one of those things? He wanted to ask so badly he had to bite his tongue. He didn't have the right. This relationship was as doomed as it had been from the beginning, but it didn't stop him from wanting.

"As painful as it's been, I've learned something from you and Amanda."

"This should be good," he joked.

"I can't run from my demons forever. Sooner or later I've got to get in touch with my mother and—" she laughed, putting a brave face on all of her troubles "—since I currently don't have other obligations, I guess now is the time."

"What about your brother?"

"I wrote him a letter after our last fight. Who knows if he'll read it, but I felt better writing it."

"I'm glad, Rachel. If there's one thing I've learned through all of this stuff with Amanda, it's that nothing goes away if you ignore it. It just gets bigger."

A lesson he was relearning right now.

Cicadas buzzed around them to create a pocket for just the two of them in the velvet night, and the feelings he'd ignored for so long grew to fill the space. He felt her against his shoulder, the slight shift of her body, and he ached to turn sideways and press her against him. Full length. Adult woman against adult man. *It had been so long....*

He took a swig of beer, mustered up his courage and lust, then turned to face Rachel. He studied her profile, the glow of her skin, the shine of her eyes. The beauty of that small, stubborn chin.

"You haven't changed," he whispered. "Not at all."

Her throat bobbed. "I hope that's not true." She looked down at the beer in her hands and her brown curls fell over her shoulder, hiding her face.

He reached up and brushed back those curls, the back of his hand grazing the velvet of her cheek. The air was charged with his intentions—they popped and crackled between them like crossed wires.

He heard her exhale and felt her breath against his palm. "You don't want to do this, Mac."

"I don't?"

She shook her head and bit her lip. "After the gratitude wears off you'll regret having touched me."

"The only thing I've ever regretted in my whole life is not touching you more." He slid his hand under her hair to her neck, and he cupped it in his palm. Felt the strength and vulnerability in it and waited for her to realize that this moment was the inevitable conclusion of her walking back into his life.

It was just as inevitable as her walking back out tomorrow. But, maybe this time they could stay friends. If such a thing was possible.

"Mac." She sighed and her head fell back until he was supporting its weight. "What are we doing?"

He smiled and stepped closer. "I'm rusty, but I think if you give me a few minutes, you'll be able to recognize it."

She laughed and turned her head to reveal emerald eyes swimming in tears. "I've missed you so much."

Not once breaking eye contact, he put their beers on the wide, flat railing. *Not once* giving her a chance to hide he leaned over her until his lips touched hers.

Just that. Her slightly chapped lips against his. Her breath against his face. The scent of her—beer and flowers—in his nose turning his brain to goo.

He pulled her as close as he could. He wrapped his arms around her so tightly that he felt the soft swell of her breasts against his fingertips, which frantically itched to touch more. Feel more. He wanted to freeze this moment, carry it with him for those years ahead when the perfection of this kiss would seem like something he might have dreamed.

Finally, just as he thought his heart would explode with all of his longing and frustration, her lips parted and her tongue touched the corner of his mouth.

"Mac."

The fire between them, held at bay for so many years, raged out of control. He wanted to pull her into his skin. He wanted to swallow her whole. He wanted to brand every inch of her with his finger-prints so that she would never again forget.

"I never forgot," she whispered, and, for a moment, he wondered if she could read his mind. But before he could say anything she attacked his mouth. She sucked his lower lip, bit it. Scraped his tongue with her teeth. Her hips pressed hard against his and he spun on his toe so she was trapped between his hard body and the railing. She lifted her hips and spread her legs on a groan as he slid forward.

Her head dropped back and he licked the hollow of her throat, the tendons that stood out against her flesh. He bit her ear, sucked on the soft skin at her collarbone until he left a mark.

Mine, the primal animal in him roared. *You've always been mine.*

She dug her fingers into his scalp, pulling at his hair until he had to lean away from her graceful, beautiful throat. She swallowed his groan with her mouth and feverishly yanked at the back of his T-shirt until it bunched up around his neck. He broke the kiss long enough to pull the thing over his head, desperate to touch more of her body with more of his.

"Look at you," she murmured. Her fingers

skimmed over him as though he had hidden messages under the surface of his aching skin and she had to find them. "Look at how beautiful you are. Mac, you're the most beaut—"

He didn't want to talk. He worried what words might spill from his own lips if given the chance. So he sealed his mouth over hers and made short work of the buttons on her green shirt. The fabric slipped and slid until he found the black lace of the bra she wore underneath it.

He brushed the tops of her breasts with the back of his hands. He looked into the endless warm green of her eyes and ran his knuckles over the hard stones of her nipples. She groaned and her eyelids fluttered.

"Look at me," he demanded. She stared at him with languid eyes. He pinched her nipples between two fingers and not once did she look away. He pulled the lace of the bra away from her skin and slid his hand into the warm pocket between lace and her breasts.

She smiled like a dazed drunk and he kissed his way over her collarbone, across the soft, sweet mound of her breast until his lips found her nipple. He rolled it between his teeth, licked it in warm welcome, and then sucked it into his mouth like a starving man.

She cried and clung to him. He lifted her, and her long legs wrapped around his waist, then he wedged her against the railing again. The pressure of the warm, hot center of her body against his erection, even through his jeans, was a luxurious pain.

He growled and released her breast to attack her mouth. His hands slid under the tight skirt she wore to cup the firm muscles of her ass through the silk of her underwear. His finger slid under elastic and found the hot, wet territory he was dying for.

She arched, her breast, damp from his mouth, pressed against his chest, and Mac knew he'd never felt anything quite as good as Rachel at this moment.

"Yes, Mac." She found his hard nipples and played thrilling, sexy games with her fingernails.

He hissed out air and spun on his heel, stumbling toward the old chaise longue that had never seen the action it was about to. His fingers brushed against her wet curls to find the hard kernel that seemed to just be waiting for him.

He laid Rachel down on the chaise and immediately pulled off the satin underwear. He pushed her skirt up and yanked her shirt off, dropping everything behind him in his haste. In short time, Rachel—hair wild, eyes hot, mouth red and damp—wore just a black bra, her skirt pushed up to her waist.

He sat across her legs and consumed the wicked, erotic sight of her.

"Mac?"

"You're all grown up, Rachel." He sighed.

"So are you," she breathed. Her hand slid up his leg and cupped him through his jeans. She pressed harder with the heel of her hand and he had to shut his eyes and think about lemons and avocados or risk putting a short end to the long night of sexual deviance he craved.

He felt her move under his legs, and soon her strong arms circled his waist and her mouth blew hot and wet against hair on the skin below his belly button.

His erection throbbed hard against the zipper of his pants.

"What do you remember about graduation night?" she asked between soft bites of his skin.

"Everything," he groaned. "I remember everything."

"I remember how you kissed me. All over."

Mac nodded, speechless, caught up in the memory of her young body's taste.

"I remember how—" her chest heaved with each breath, her breasts trembled over the black bra "—shocked and scared I was by what you did to me. How you touched me." She took one of his hands and placed it on her thigh and slowly pushed it toward her gorgeous sex. But it was you. Mac. My very best friend. So, I let it happen and it was amazing."

"You felt so good. You still do." His hand gripped the muscle in her leg, and then he brushed the back of his hand gently across the curls between her legs. One finger eased slightly deeper into her.

"You touched me as if I was precious." She moaned, jerking slightly when his finger found her clitoris again.

He cupped her face in his other hand. "You are. You always have been."

"You're the only person in my life who ever made me believe that," she confessed, and he groaned, destroyed by what she'd said.

He kissed her hard, trying to make her understand everything that she did to him, with her body and her mind and her words and her heart.

She broke the kiss, panting hard, and one of her hands started to work on his zipper. "You touched me as if I might break."

"It was our first time. I thought *I* might break."

She smiled, her beautiful face glowing. He leaned down to kiss her just as her hand eased into his boxers to grip him, and he had to rest his head against her forehead to catch his breath. Her thumb circled the end of his penis.

"I'm not going to break." She pushed his pants down over his hips. "But let's see how you do." He caught her dirty grin just before she eased him into her mouth.

The thirteen years between them burned up in the night. The chaise longue collapsed during the execution of one of Mac's particular fantasies. And in the end, Mac did break. It had been years for him. Long, lonely years. But Rachel was right behind him, her body a vise around his. Her cries a sweet echo in his head.

"WELL, MAC EDWARDS, YOU haven't missed a beat." She patted his sweaty, heaving stomach.

"I'm thirty, Rachel." He stroked her shoulder with his hand. "Hardly an old man." But her compliment lit a little fire of vanity in his chest. It's nice to be compared favorably to a seventeen-year-old boy, even if that seventeen-year-old boy had been him.

The arm Rachel used as a pillow was losing feeling, but he didn't want to move. If they moved, stopped touching, the night would be over. Which meant it was tomorrow and he had to say goodbye to her. So he let his arm go numb, and he let the sweat cool on his body and wished he had some kind of power over time.

She sighed and kissed his cheek, settling deeper into the side of his body.

"Do you have splinters?" He shifted and swept a hand under his butt, checking for injury.

"Probably." She sighed. "Is that the sun?" She pointed into the brightening eastern sky.

"I think so," he murmured, counting his losses, suturing his wounds so he could go on after she left. "Do you want to stay?" Her head jerked and he could feel her stare at him. "I mean, it's a long drive and it's late—"

"Early," she whispered.

"Right." He smiled at her, trying to pretend as if the flesh wasn't being torn from his heart. "So?"

She pushed up on her elbow and hugged his chest, her hair spilling over his skin. "You're asking me to spend the night so I can wake up in a few hours and do this all over again? How can I say no?"

She leaned down to kiss him, but he dodged her. Was she nuts? Had she forgotten his mother? His promises to never put Amanda through that?

"Rachel, we wouldn't be in the same room. I'll give you my bed and I'll sleep on the couch." Rachel sat up next to him and they both watched the sky turn pink. "I can't confuse Amanda right now. I can't—"

"This is about your mom, isn't it?" Rachel asked.

Mac shrugged. "A little, maybe. But mostly it's about Amanda." He found his underwear and started to pull it on. She put a hand on his arm and stopped him.

"I understand, Mac. It's all right."

She looked young in the hazy light of dawn. Naked and fresh and new, as she had the night of graduation... Just before she'd ripped the rug out from under his world.

This isn't a second chance, he told himself as he stroked the satin of her cheek one last time.

CHAPTER FOURTEEN

RACHEL AWOKE TO AN ACHE between her legs. A slight tenderness and pulling in her thighs that had not been there in a long, long time. She smiled, half-awake, and rolled onto her back on unfamiliar sheets in a strange bed surrounded by the sunshine and pine-tree smell of Mac.

Mac.

Her eyes popped open.

That explained the ache.

And the permagrin.

She pulled the worn white sheets up to her nose and took a deep breath.

Mac.

She dropped the sheet and her arms flopped down to her sides. If she had been the giggling type, she would have giggled up at the pale gold ceiling. She could have burst into song, talked to birds, climbed every mountain.

There should be more musicals, she thought. Which was ludicrous since, as a rule, she hated musicals. But not this morning. This morning with her Mac-ache and covered in Mac-scent she understood how spontaneous song might be the only way to express the sheer volume of joy in her body. *Too bad I don't know how to tap-dance.*

Of course, it would have been so much better to wake up to a little more Mac, but she understood his concern. Well, she understood why he had that concern.

Watching his mother's parade of boyfriends had been devastating to Mac growing up. And she understood why he wanted to shield Amanda from that experience. Mac didn't seem to understand that it wasn't the boyfriends that had damaged him—for the most part, they'd been good men. It was the way his mother had handled it. Mac could have control of this situation, explain it in such a way that Amanda didn't feel threatened and Rachel could help. She could—

What am I thinking? She chewed her lip. *I am not thinking. Not anymore.*

Her entire life had been dictated by what she'd thought was best. She'd put away her emotional compass when she'd left Mac the first time and now she had to dig it out of storage.

She held her breath, cleared her mind and waited for her first feeling, an indicator of what she wanted and how she should act.

Hope filled her like helium in a balloon until she was sure she floated over Mac's bed.

Last night was the start of something. A second chance. She knew it.

She turned her head to gaze out the window at the green treetops that swayed in the wind against the bright blue sky.

Imagine that view every morning. Imagine this bed, these sheets. Mac. Every day. Imagine I get the right to him again. And to Amanda. I get to call them mine.

She smiled and shut her eyes, squeezing back the tears that she didn't want to fall.

She'd taken those steps over the cliff sometime in the night. Whether it had been at the station, or later when she followed Mac onto the porch knowing full well what would happen in the moonlight, she didn't know. But now she was airborne, flying, and it had been years since she'd felt this good.

She kicked off her sheets and ran her hands over Mac's T-shirt, which he'd given her to wear to bed. It was gray and worn and soft and she was pretty sure, no matter what the day might bring, that she wouldn't be giving it back to Mac.

She pulled on her underwear and her skirt, and with her heart in her throat and wings on her feet, she pulled open the bedroom door and went to find her second chance.

Mac and Amanda were in the kitchen. Or what used to be the kitchen. From her vantage point on the landing it looked like the scene of a flour explosion. Mac was doubled over at the sink, laughing so hard tears made tracks through the white powder on his face.

"Great idea, Amanda. Really," he said, using his T-shirt to wipe his face. "These are going to be excellent pancakes."

"Well, how was I supposed to know the bag was going to split apart like that?"

Rachel sucked in air, surprised by the warm tone of Amanda's voice.

"Maybe we'd better just stick to bacon," Mac suggested, sweeping a mound of flour into his hand. A plate of bacon cooled on a paper towel next to his elbow.

"But, Rachel—" Amanda started.

"Loves bacon," Rachel interrupted, and Amanda whirled, her face alight with flour and the happiness she'd been without for so long.

Mac didn't look up from his careful sweeping of the counter.

"Rachel! We were going to make breakfast for you, but—" Amanda shrugged and looked at her bright red shirt that appeared pink thanks to the fine coat of white powder "—we had an accident."

"Looks like it." Rachel stepped into the kitchen, watching Mac out of the corner of her eye as he did everything but acknowledge her.

Stones rolled in her stomach.

"How did you sleep?" Amanda asked, her voice a cheerful distraction.

"Like a rock. How about you?"

"Same."

"How did you sleep, Mac?" Rachel asked. *Look at me. Look at me, Mac.*

"Just fine, thanks." He dumped a handful of flour in the garbage and washed his hands at the sink, all with his back to her. "You need to get to school, young lady. You better go on upstairs and change."

Amanda ran past Rachel with a big smile and launched herself up the stairs.

"Mac," she said as soon as Amanda was out of earshot. "What's wrong—"

"We can talk about it when Amanda leaves." His voice was ice, sliding into her veins and chilling her to the bone. He started spreading peanut butter on wheat bread, folded it over and put bacon in the middle.

"All right, guys!" Amanda ran back down the stairs, wearing a different red T-shirt. She grabbed her backpack from the landing and swung it over her shoulder, then launched herself at her father, grabbing the peanut-butter-and-bacon sandwich he held out to her while she let herself be kissed by him.

She then turned to Rachel, who stood frozen in grief and anxiety, and looped an arm around Rachel's waist and squeezed. "See you after school," she said, flinging herself up the stairs like a regular kid.

"Amanda, you probably won't see—" Mac

started, but Rachel interrupted, unwilling to give Mac the opportunity to end things this way. In front of his daughter. Without a fight.

"See you, Amanda." She waved and the door slammed shut behind the girl. Rachel turned on Mac, ready to fight.

"She's a totally different girl," Mac said, continuing his cleanup as if there wasn't an electrical storm between them. "I can't believe the changes."

"Mac—"

"I mean, I'm not sure if I've ever seen her as happy as she was this morning. She wanted to make pancakes…." He shook his head. "Yesterday morning I couldn't even get her to drink a glass of milk."

Rachel stepped into the kitchen, around the island, and got in front of Mac while he wiped down the counters. "Are you pretending nothing happened?" she asked.

"Rachel." He sighed and hung his head, still unable to look at her. "I'm not pretending anything."

She felt sick. Used. "Oh? So this is how you treat all your lovers the morning after? Like strangers?"

"I don't have lovers, Rachel." His eyes scorched her skin, dried her out and turned her into a desert. "I had you and Margaret. So you'll have to excuse me if I don't know how to do this."

"What is *this,* Mac? Is this your payback for thirteen years ago?"

"No!" he said, fast and fierce. Finally his eyes met

hers and she reeled from the pain in the blue depths. "No, this…" He rubbed at his face. "This is a mess."

"You're going to have to do better than that, Mac. If you expect me to just walk out of here like…" She couldn't finish the thought. *Like I didn't want more. Oh, my God, am I such a fool?*

"Are trying to say that you'd stay? Who are you kidding, Rachel? New Springs is a noose around your neck, remember?"

"I want to try."

"Try what?" Mac asked. He stepped away from her and cold air rushed in where his heat had been. "Dating? You want to date?"

She shrugged, no longer airborne but crawling through the ruins of her stupid fantasies. "Why not?"

"Why not?" His laughter was manic. "Because you live in Santa Barbara—"

"It's thirty minutes away, Mac. Not the other side of the world."

He nodded. "Okay, fine, but stretch this out. We date, then what? This is my land, Rachel. I can't leave here. You think you're going to move here? Meet me for dinner at the Main Street Café? What about your mom? What about your brother?"

"I told you, Mac. I am going to deal with it."

"Oh." His sarcastic laugh abraded her skin. "That should be good. I give you ten minutes with her before you're running for the door."

His opinion of her stung.

"You're one to talk, since I'm not the one running for the door right now."

He looked so sad, like a man resigned to his spot on the cross. He studied the flour on his hands but didn't say anything.

This second chance was slipping through her fingers. Tears flooded Rachel's eyes. "I've missed you so much, Mac."

His jaw tensed. "I've missed you, too, but I have a daughter to think of. And I want you to be in our lives, but it can't be in that way. Not now."

"You're never going to date again so that Amanda never has to share you with anyone? That doesn't make any sense."

"It makes perfect sense." His hands fisted on the counter. "It makes sense for my family, right now. Nothing is more important than Amanda. Not you, and definitely not me."

Rachel could only blink. "You're being unreasonable."

Mac shook his head. "Maybe, but it's my decision."

But what about me? she wanted to say. "What about us?"

His blue eyes bored into hers. "You made sure there was no us thirteen years ago, Rachel. I begged you to give me a second chance and you said no. You said you never wanted to see me again." His words were daggers, ice picks, and she had to shut her eyes so the pain wouldn't kill her. "That was our second chance, Rachel."

"So what was last night?"

"Last night?" He stared at his hands instead of at her. "I think last night was a mistake."

She turned away from him, gripping the counter as hard as she could, trying to find reality in all this madness.

"I'm sorry, Rachel." She felt him behind her and she jerked away before he could touch her. Anger bolstered her, filled her lungs and turned her bones to steel, her heart to stone.

"You're a coward, Mac Edwards. This is not about you protecting your daughter. It's about you being scared I'll leave you again." She whirled to face him. His beauty was salt in the wound but she still watched him, still soaked him in with her eyes. "I'm not going anywhere, Mac. I'm here and I'm staying—"

"But Amanda—"

"You talk to your daughter, Mac. You're short-changing her and you're robbing us of the chance to be happy."

"You don't know that that's even possible. We have a past and we had great sex. Maybe that's all we've got."

She shook her head, picking herself up from the ashes. She'd never once fought for what she wanted, she constantly ran away from what she didn't want. Well, that was going to change. "I've never loved

anyone my whole life the way I love you. I loved you
when we were sixteen and I didn't know what to do
with it, so I threw it away. Well, this time I know
what to do and I'm not going to let you throw me
away. Talk to your daughter. Give us a chance."

"Maybe I don't want a chance." He was different,
somehow, angrier, though there was no indication of
it other than what she could feel in the air around
him. Blame. "You're asking me to take a big risk,
Rachel. Tear apart my family, hurt my little girl, all
so you can leave me again?"

Rachel crossed the three steps between them. She
cupped his face in her hands, and when he pulled away
she held him tighter. "I was a scared kid from a crappy
home," she said, willing the words into his brain, his
gut, his better sense. "I didn't trust you, I didn't trust
myself, and I am more sorry than I can say that I hurt
you. I have spent every moment the past thirteen years
distancing myself from other people so I would never
hurt anyone or be hurt like that again. And I am tired
of it. I want to feel again. I want to be in love, and if I
end up hurt, it's okay. It's worth it. Because I love you."

She didn't know if it worked, if he really heard
her, but he no longer struggled to escape, and so she
took advantage of his closeness and leaned up on her
toes to kiss him. It took him a while, a stupid moment
of pretending to be unaffected, but then he pulled her
into his arms and lifted her off her feet. She poured
everything she had into that kiss, every foolish dream

she'd never given herself the chance to dream. Every desire, want and missed chance. Every lonely Friday night, every date she went on just so she wouldn't sit at home and drown herself in work.

And Mac took all of that and returned it. Until his hand was up her skirt and she was half reclined over the island.

"Mac," she groaned. She pushed his shoulder away and he dropped her like a hot potato. He spun away from her, fisted his hands in his shaggy hair.

"I don't know what to do," he whispered.

His confusion and pain hurt her more than his anger. Another sure indicator that this feeling eating away at her organs was love. "I do."

She eased off the counter and pressed a hand to her bruised and swollen mouth. If she didn't leave now, she'd stay and they'd make love with all of this anger and uncertainty between them and they would both get sliced to ribbons.

She grabbed her bags and walked away from Mac on trembling legs.

"I'm staying, Mac," she said. "I'll be at my mother's."

He let her go without saying a word.

RACHEL, SHATTERED AND fragile, watched the paint chips flutter and flake off her mother's house and sincerely questioned her sanity.

She should come back some other day, perhaps.

Certainly not the day after she'd lost her job and definitely not moments after being kicked in the heart by the only man she ever loved.

Perfect! A fine time to reunite with my mother.

Rachel rested her head against the steering wheel and took a look around at her emotional rock bottom.

No place to go but up. She tried to rally herself, but it didn't work. She sighed and rolled her head to look out her window at the ruins of her childhood house.

Her mother stood on the porch watching her.

Rachel's heart stopped and her eyes burned with surprising tears.

Mom, what happened to you? The thirteen years since she'd last seen Eve sat upon her mother's thick, curved shoulders, and had carved her face into unforgiving lines. Her hair, so black and thick in Rachel's memory, was mostly silver now.

Eve lifted her cigarette to her mouth, and after a moment she exhaled and shrouded herself in a veil of smoke. That at least was familiar. The gray fog of her bad habit had always obscured Eve.

Hello, Mom.

Rachel put her keys in her purse and hauled her body out of her car. She forced her lead feet to take her across the street and up the broken sidewalk that split the overgrown lawn. But she stopped at the steps to the sagging porch.

"Well, well," Eve said, her voice like sandpaper

against Rachel's bruised spirit. "Look what the wind finally blew in."

"Hello." Rachel's voice was a rasp, and she stopped, having exhausted her conversational skills.

"Lots of people seem to be hanging around this house these days." She took another drag of the smoke. "You need money?" Eve asked, and Rachel mustered a reluctant smile. As if she'd go to her mom for money.

Rachel shook her head.

Eve nodded and smoked while Rachel watched her, fighting the magnetic push and pull inside of her. Leave. Stay. Run. Fight.

"I heard you was in town, working with Mac and that girl of his."

It was Rachel's turn to nod, unable to break out of this surreal scene. She didn't know what would happen if she opened her mouth, if years of poison and spite would fly from her lips. So she kept her mouth shut and let her mother awkwardly steer them through these strange waters.

"Did it work? You put that girl's head right?"

Rachel nodded again, and after a moment Eve laughed, a growling grumble that turned quickly into a chest-shuddering cough.

"Well, I can't say I know why you're here. But if you want to stay out here gabbing all day we can, or you can come in and have a coffee. I'm for coffee." Eve turned, her Main Street Café uniform pulled tight across her sturdy hips. Her long silver-streaked hair hung to her waist like a curtain.

Once upon a time Rachel used to comb her mother's hair. Endlessly. They had played beauty parlor when she was a little girl, and Eve had let Rachel put her hair up in curlers and braids, French twists and pigtails.

"It's beautiful," her mother had said one of the last times they'd played. She had preened in the dirty bathroom mirror. "Perfect for the ball."

"That'll be a million dollars," Rachel had joked, holding out her eight-year-old palm, her pockets filled with bobby pins.

"Highway robbery!" Eve had gasped. "But I'll give you a million kisses." Eve had swooped down and pulled Rachel into her strong arms, against her big, soft chest, and peppered her head and face with kisses until, Rachel, laughing and breathless, had said that was enough.

"Never enough," Eve had sighed against her hair. "Never enough kisses."

"Mom," Rachel said, and Eve turned around, her creased face lifted into surprise. *I'm sorry,* was on the tip of Rachel's tongue, but those were the wrong words. Those were easy words that would make all this awkwardness go away, but the truth was, she wasn't sorry.

Dad says sometimes people do things that hurt other people without knowing it. They do it because they're hurting, too.

Rachel didn't feel strong enough to let go of all that hurt and anger. What would keep her upright? If she absolved her mother Rachel was sure she would deflate until all that remained was the empty bag of her skin.

Is that all I am? she wondered. *All I've got is bitterness?*

The thought made her sick. No wonder Mac wasn't ready to take another chance on her. What good did she have to give him when everything was crowded out by spite?

"You weren't a very good mother," she finally said.

Eve nodded. "You think I don't know that?"

"But I forgive you." Rachel had to catch herself on the wobbly porch railing as everything she'd held so tightly for so long leaked out of her. "Hear me, Mom?" she said, and started to laugh. "I forgive you."

"Well." Eve's throat bobbed as she swallowed, and her dark eyes watered. "Sure I hear you, the whole town can hear you." She turned to the front door, and as she did, Rachel grabbed her mother's callused hand.

And Eve gripped it hard, not letting go.

CHAPTER FIFTEEN

THE SUNLIGHT LEECHED FROM Amanda's face.

"What do you mean Rachel's gone?" she asked, and dropped her book bag by the door with a heavy thunk. "When's she coming back?"

"I don't know, Amanda," Mac answered. He had not expected this sudden storm from the girl who had skipped out of the house this morning, but maybe he should have. No other woman had spent the night in their home and Amanda was bound to think something about it.

Rachel never should have stayed.

He finished wiping his hands and looped the tea towel through the refrigerator door handle. He was going to start telling the truth, no matter how hard. "I don't know if she'll ever be back."

"Ever?" Amanda wailed.

"Amanda." He was puzzled by this vehement response. "She wasn't going to be here forever. She was just here for counseling—"

"But I thought she was your friend."

"She was…she…" God, this wasn't easy. "She is my friend, but she lives in Santa Barbara and she's busy and has a job and…" Amanda's face was turning to stone again. The brief glimpse of his daughter that he'd had this morning was vanishing right in front of his eyes. Panic tap danced on his nerve endings. "I know you like her, but she—"

She laughed, but it was like black blood welling up from an old wound. "You don't know shit, Dad."

He reeled for a second, smacked by her language and her bile. "Amanda." He took a step toward her, but she ran away from him up the stairs. The door to her room slammed shut with such force that all the windows shook.

He needed to deal with his daughter's disrespect and language, her sudden and terrible turn of attitude. He had to forget Rachel and pretend as though last night had never happened. He needed to figure out how to get her job back for her and repair some of the damage that had been done.

He had to get on with his life. Right now. This minute or he'd fall apart.

Mac collapsed onto the bottom step and cradled his head in his hands.

"What am I supposed to do?" he whispered to the ghosts that surrounded him. The ghost of his angry, unhappy wife. The ghost of his daughter, laughing and covered in flour. And the ghost of Rachel, loving him in a way he'd forgotten was possible.

A pendulum swung in his chest, away from Rachel and then, moments later, right back to her.

He shouldn't have slept with her, that much was obvious. Making love to her had only made the whole mess worse. He'd known it last night but had ignored that in his lust. It was, after all, the one thing he could count on—giving into his feelings for Rachel would only bring him pain.

And now he had Amanda's pain to deal with.

He groaned and rubbed his face.

The only woman he'd ever loved and she was the only person who could rip apart his life with such precision.

Although this time, he wasn't the only one left in need of some repair. She'd lost her job over him and Amanda.

I chose you.

He didn't know what he could do to be worthy of that, but he had to do something.

AMANDA SCRATCHED AT HER SKIN. The bees were back. She could feel them in the muscles of her arms and she dug hard at her wrists. If she could just break the skin, then the bees would get out and she could be normal again.

Dad pulled the truck to a stop in front of Grandma and Grandpa's house and the seat bounced under her as the engine idled.

Normal. As if she even knew what that was. She'd

thought things would get back to normal after last night—it had felt so good to tell Christie's secret. She'd opened her mouth and the bees had flown out, and she'd been able, for a few hours, to remember what it was like before all the secrets.

But then Dad had to ruin it all.

Now all the secrets built up inside her and wanted out. Everything. Mom. The accident. But if Amanda said anything, it would kill Dad.

"I'll be back in a few hours," Dad said as he stretched his arm across the top of the seat and pulled on the end of her long ponytail. She stopped herself from jerking away, just in time. "Do you have any homework?"

"It's Friday night, Dad."

He nodded, and she knew he wouldn't press the subject. She'd hurt him earlier when she swore at him and now he was giving her space before he'd try and sit her down for some big heart-to-heart talk about how they had to be good to each other, because there was only the two of them.

Yeah, and whose fault is that?

"Well, when I get back we'll see if you can beat your old man at chess."

"Where are you going?" she asked.

"I'm going to Santa Barbara."

"Are you going to see Rachel?" She scratched at her arm through her long-sleeved T-shirt.

"I don't think so. Why are you so worried?"

"You shouldn't keep secrets, Dad," she said, and then scooted out of the truck and walked toward the front door where Grandma stood waving.

"CAN YOU POINT ME TO Olivia Hernandez's office?" Mac asked one of the women sitting behind the hive of cubicles in the center of the DCFS offices. He thought he knew the way, but one corner looked the same as the next in these government buildings.

"Just around that corner," the woman told him with a bright but harried smile.

"Thanks," he said, taking the left turn as she'd directed and locating the brass nameplate on Olivia's door.

He took a deep breath and knocked, trying to control his temper that had simmered and boiled over the long drive to the city.

"Come on in!"

Mac eased open the door to see the small Hispanic spitfire sitting behind piles of files. At the sight of him her eyes went wide and she sat back, her chair rolling away from her computer.

"Well, well, if it isn't the man of the hour."

Mac's eye twitched out of nerves. *Is she joking? Should I laugh?*

"Come on in." She gestured to one of the rickety, narrow chairs in front of her desk.

"Thank you," he said, and though he'd much rather stand, he folded himself into the chair.

"I understand there's been an arrest in your daughter's case." Olivia folded her hands over her tiny belly but still somehow managed to look like the Godfather. "That must be quite a relief."

He nodded. "It was…is. Yes, thank you."

The silence in the room stretched and Mac looked at his hands. His frustration grew with every breath, like a fire. He felt powerless and weak against all that had happened. And the last thing he wanted was to cause Rachel more trouble.

"I am guessing you are here for a reason?" Olivia asked, her eyebrows high on her forehead.

"I want Rachel Filmore to get her job back." The words erupted from him as if under their own power.

Olivia blinked. Blinked again. "She resigned."

"She was *forced* to resign."

She shrugged. "Anywhere else, with any other boss, she would have been fired. I'd say she got off lucky considering the rules she'd broken."

"Why? Because we were friends a million years ago?"

"Mac, I cannot discuss this with you. You must understand that. Rachel resigned, there is nothing I can do." She held her hands out as if to prove how powerless she was.

Mac stood, bristling with thwarted anger. "That woman saved my daughter. She saved my family, and it's one screwed-up place that rewards her hard work with unemployment." He turned to go, so disgusted he didn't know what to do with himself.

"Oh, sit down," Olivia said, as though he was a kid throwing a tantrum.

"Why?" He bit the word out.

"Because I want to know the guy my friend and my best counselor gave up her career for."

The words hit him in the chest and stopped his heart. *I chose you.* Rachel's words haunted him.

He leaned against the door but didn't sit, waiting.

"Rachel has one rule in her life and that is to never get attached," Olivia said. "She has boyfriends, but she doesn't keep them. She doesn't talk to her family, even though her mother lives less than an hour away. I thought I was her only friend and then you come along." Olivia cocked her head and stared at him as if determining his worth. "And Rachel breaks her golden rule—she jeopardizes the only thing she's got in her life, her job, all for you. So, I've got a question for you. Why are you here? Really."

Mac blinked, surprised by the question. "I want to get her her job back. It's the least I can do."

Olivia watched him for a long time with a gaze that penetrated Mac's skin and saw through his anger and irrational frustration. Mac tried to hide all of his feelings for Rachel from those spotlight eyes. He tried to push his tangled emotions down so that this clever woman wouldn't see them in his face or eyes or stance.

"You're lying." Olivia said, despite Mac's

efforts. "There's a whole lot more going on here than gratitude."

I've never loved anyone my whole life the way I love you.

He shook his head to shake Rachel's words from his memory.

"How about if you unclench your teeth before you break your jaw and try telling me the truth," Olivia suggested.

Mac bit down harder on his back teeth.

She sighed. "You two deserve each other. I've never met two harder heads in my life."

"Then you understand I won't give up on Rachel getting her job back."

"Wow." She shook her head. "You are both stubborn and stupid."

"Wait a second..." Anger leaped again.

She held up her hand. "Billy Martinez called me with concerns that Rachel was playing house with a family that needed a counselor, not a pretend mother."

Family. The word was beguiling, a dream, smoke far too thin to be real.

"He was imagining things."

"And I guess I imagined the fireworks that went off in my office a few weeks ago when you were here?"

Mac blushed and looked at his hands again.

"I've never seen Rachel the way she's been the past month. If it were any other situation, I'd be turning cartwheels that some man managed to get

under her armor. But right now I am more concerned
for her state of mind and well-being. So, how about
you stop with the righteous indignation and tell me
what's really going on?" Olivia asked quietly.

*I've loved her since the moment I saw her in
freshman science class.* But he denied it; after all, he
was good at it. It was second nature, the easiest thing
in the world.

He shook his head. "I have to get Rachel her job
back and protect Amanda. That's it. That's all that's
important."

"Protect Amanda from what?"

"What do you mean from what? From being hurt."

Olivia's smile was sad, and it reached deep into
his chest and settled around his heart. "You are not
going to be able to get Rachel's job back. She made
a choice and the choice was you. And you're not
going to be able to protect your daughter from being
hurt. It's impossible. I've got two girls that I would
surround in bubble wrap and lock in their rooms if I
could." She pressed her hands to her chest, her eyes
dark pools of understanding. "But I can't. You are
going to need some new goals."

"There are no other goals." Things were breaking
inside of him, walls and support beams were crum-
bling from this woman's sudden compassion and
surprising warmth.

"What about you?" she asked. "What do you want?
You're thirty years old and your high school girl-

friend walks back into your life. You're clearly as involved as Rachel is. Are you going to just let all that go?"

Mac rubbed his face and turned to the small window with the view of another government building. It said something about Olivia that he wasn't walking away from these personal questions.

"You're good," he told her with a small smile and a sideways glance.

"So I'm told." She smiled back, and Mac decided he would like this woman, like her a lot, if she hadn't fired Rachel. "But you're also a man who's got something on his mind."

"No kidding." He sighed. His brain was like a gerbil on one of those wheels. He couldn't get off thoughts of Rachel; they spun faster and faster beneath his feet.

"What's the problem, Mac?" Olivia stood and walked around her desk to perch on the front.

He held his breath. "Is this how it works with all those teenagers and families you work with? You lure them into your office and get them to spill their guts?" He tried to laugh off how much he wanted to spill his guts.

She shrugged. "The sad truth of my job is that I can only help people who want help. If they keep all their secrets and problems to themselves, I can't do anything for them."

Mac collapsed into the chair opposite her and gave up the fight.

"I don't think I can survive another woman walking out on me. Especially Rachel." He laughed, but it hurt. "Again."

"You can't spend your whole life planning for disappointment. It's faith, Mac. That's all love is. It's taking the leap every day and hoping the other person will be there to catch you every day."

"I tried that once," he said with a grim smile. "It didn't work so well."

"Then it wasn't love."

God. Is it that simple?

Mac thought of Rachel's face the day he'd surprised her here. She had not been happy. Mac smiled. That day had been the beginning of the end for him, he realized now. If he'd been able to hold her off with all of his anger and bitterness, he might not be in this spot. But when she'd turned those green eyes on him and apologized and told him he had to trust her, all his resistance ebbed out like a tide.

"Rachel's changed, Mac. I think you and your daughter changed her."

Mac's wheezy huff sounded from his chest. When she'd first walked into his house three weeks ago she'd looked like a pickled version of herself, a woman so uptight she could barely bend to sit down. But this morning... He sighed. This morning she was a different woman. Loose, happy, at least until he'd put an end to that.

She'd had the courage to change, to reach out to him and he—

"I am such a chickenshit," he confessed.

Olivia laughed. "I doubt that." Mac raised an eyebrow. "It takes a lot of courage to get up every day and do what you've done. Talk to your daughter. She's a smart girl. She obviously likes Rachel and she obviously trusts her. That's the groundwork, Mac. It's up to you to build on that, and if Rachel's no longer your counselor, there's nothing to stop you." Olivia eyed Mac and then winked.

Nothing to stop you.

The dream of Rachel, of having a life with her, was so beguiling he couldn't actually hold the thought in his head without wanting to break into a tribal victory dance.

Was this possible? Could he do it? Could she?

The weight on his shoulders lifted. The ropes of worry and fear around his neck that dragged him down and stopped him from reaching for things he'd desired eased. Loosened.

"Just talk to her, huh? That doesn't go so well for me these days."

"Try, Mac, that's all you can do."

He knew that, but maybe it was time to try for something new. The old stuff—trying to pretend everything was normal, that he wasn't lonely—clearly wasn't working.

Time to stop pretending.

"I gotta get back." Mac pushed out of the chair. "I'm sorry for how I came in here—"

"Don't worry.' Olivia clapped him on the shoulder as she walked him to the door. "You're lucky I didn't take you out back and teach you a lesson."

He smiled at the small but tough woman. "I imagine you would have, too."

Olivia laughed, and Mac, feeling loose and, frankly, disconnected from the stones of responsibility and duty, pulled her into a big hug.

"Thanks," he whispered.

"Just doing my job," she whispered back. "Now, get out of here before I call Security." She returned to her desk and sat, back in Godfather mode.

He dug his keys out of his pocket. "Thanks. Now I understand why Rachel was so scared of you."

She grinned and Mac nearly ran out in his haste. He deserved happiness. So did Rachel, and he was going to ensure that they had it.

THE TRUCK WASN'T EVEN IN Park before George McCormick was out the front door, one of his goofy Hawaiian shirts fluttering in the breeze behind him.

All of Mac's easiness vanished, replaced by panic. "What's wrong?" he asked, trotting up to the older man, meeting him on the lawn.

"Nothing." George held out his hands. "Nothing. Well." He winced. "Your daughter is fine, but she's been acting a little strange since she got here."

"Strange?" Mac asked with trepidation. *Strange* was a terrible iceberg word, only so much revealed and a world of trouble hidden.

George turned back toward his house and Mac fell into step beside him. "She's gotten out all of Margaret's pictures. I swear, she went into the attic by herself and got out a box of stuff that we'd forgotten we even had."

The flighty, awkward hope that he'd been nurturing during the drive back took a nosedive.

"What's she doing with it? Is she okay?"

"She's just going through it. She keeps asking us questions…." George shook his head. "Cindy's with her now, but I'm telling you, she's like a girl possessed."

The tethers to the stones of duty and the past slithered up his legs, across his gut and circled his chest. "She had a rough day yesterday," Mac said.

Understatement of the century.

"She told us a little." George nodded. "She said Rachel Filmore spent the night."

Mac stopped and dug his thumbs into his eyes, trying to relieve the sudden pain there. *Of everything she could say, of all the things that had happened,* that's *what she chooses to talk about?*

"You okay, Mac?"

"I guess I'll find out in a few minutes."

They walked through the open door into the cool house. "She's in the den," George told him, and Mac turned into the warm, book-lined room. Mac had tutored Margaret in this room a million years ago. He'd shown up with books and worksheets, and the hard-hearted determination to make Rachel jealous. But Margaret had shown no interest in molecular biology. She had locked the door and introduced him to the joys of oral sex. And for weeks afterward he couldn't look Rachel in the eyes, because as he'd sat back and let it happen, he had pretended it was Rachel's mouth on him.

The memory of that night, the ghosts of those two girls, of the boy he had been, whispered in his ears: *You'll never be free of us.*

His daughter sat like a pink-and-blond island surrounded by all of Margaret's old dolls, a tangle of gymnastic ribbons and her school photos. His past, his present and future were all twisted around Rachel, Margaret and Amanda. Mac longed to fall down on the ground and wail his grief and confusion into the brown shag carpet.

"Hi, Mac," Cindy said, her voice cheerful but her eyes serious and wary. "We're just going through some of Margaret's old stuff."

"I see that. Amanda?" His daughter looked up at him with old eyes. "What have you found?"

She shrugged that hateful, blithe one-shouldered half lift. He stepped over a stack of photo albums and sat down next to her. She scooted away.

"Have you eaten?"

"I'm not hungry."

He caught Cindy's eyes over his daughter's head. They were damp and he felt an answering bite in his own. "I'm starved," he said, his voice gruff despite the cheer he forced into it.

"I'll go check the pot roast." Cindy stood and left the room.

"And I," George said, "will go set up the chessboard so my granddaughter can embarrass me in front of my son-in-law."

George paused in the doorway, his face lit with the hope that Amanda might say something, tease him the way she had a few short weeks ago. But she only flipped the page in the photo album she studied. George left and the silence between Mac and his daughter hurt.

"Amanda?"

"What?" She flipped another page.

"What are you looking at?"

She pushed the album off her knees so Mac could see it. In the corner picture Margaret shoved a piece of wedding cake into Mac's mouth. He wore a black suit and she had on a lace dress with flowers—pink ones, lovely and delicate—in her hair.

"Wow," he said. "She was pretty that day, huh?"

Amanda didn't say anything.

This isn't working. Pretending everything is okay has failed. I have to try something new.

Mac took a deep breath and all of his courage in hand. "Amanda, please look at me. I want to talk to you."

She turned a little and looked as far as his chest, which would have to suffice. "You know I love you, don't you?"

"Sure."

"And I think most of the time you like me." He leaned down to see how she might react to his sad attempt at humor. She didn't. "Well, we're it. We're all that's left of the Edwards family, so we have to be good to each other. We have to be kind. Do you get where I am going?"

"I'm sorry I swore at you today," she muttered.

"Thank you. Can you tell me why you're so mad? Can you…" She looked away and turned another page in the album. Mac turned his eyes heavenward and prayed for patience. "Is it about Mom?"

He waited for her standard screaming "Not everything is about Mom!" response, but none came. "Is that why you're going through her things?"

No response. Just the beat of his heart in his ears.

"Do you want to talk about Rachel?"

Her eyes shot up to his and he held his breath, hoping for…something. Resolution. An end to this walking on eggshells business. But she didn't say anything.

Well, he thought, his breath shuddery and heavy. *No time like the present.*

"I would like to talk about Rachel," he said. "I know you—"

"Did you really love Mom?" Amanda asked, out of the blue.

Mac shook his head, positive he had mental whiplash. "What?"

"Did you really love her? I know she was pregnant with me when you got married, so it's not like you got married because you wanted to—"

"Amanda." He grabbed her tiny shoulder, feeling all too clearly the shift of bone under her skin. He eased his desperate grip, worried he'd been too rough with his fragile daughter. "I wanted to get married because I loved your mother and we both loved you. We didn't plan for you, but you were the best thing that happened to us." It was a white lie, one that he'd told a thousand times, but what could it hurt? He didn't love Margaret, but he'd grown to care before that, too, turned black with her ongoing deceptions and betrayals. Yet he'd always loved his daughter. From the moment Margaret came to him to tell him the news he'd been in love with his child.

She laughed, a skeptical huff.

"You don't believe me?"

"I believe that you wanted me, but I am pretty sure she could have cared less."

"Is this because of the time she left?" She didn't answer for a long time. "Amanda, that wasn't about you. That was about Mom and me. She loved you very much and I—" His voice caught and his eyes filled with tears. "You're my life, kiddo."

"Do you think Mom loved you?" she asked, her voice so cold he felt a chill in his gut.

He nodded. "Absolutely. I just don't think it was as easy as she thought it was going to be. But absolutely, your mother and I loved each other and we loved you very much."

This was the opposite of his plan. He was supposed to stop pretending. He was supposed to be trying something new, but he couldn't. His daughter's doubt terrified him and he didn't have the courage.

Amanda's gaze fell to the picture album in her lap and Mac's followed. "Look at us," he said, pointing to the picture of them with the cake. "You can practically hear her laughing."

"I don't remember her laugh anymore," Amanda said.

"Well, it was a good one. Until she really got going and started to snort, then it was pretty ugly."

Amanda smiled and Mac closed his eyes in thanks for that small curl to his daughter's lips.

"What did you want to say about Rachel?" Amanda asked as she shut the photo album.

Mac faltered. He wasn't proud of it, but he told himself it was the right thing to do. For Amanda. For his family.

"Nothing," he said. He helped his daughter put away the tattered and musty remnants of his wife's childhood.

CHAPTER SIXTEEN

RACHEL STOOD IN THE DARK hallway outside her childhood bedroom. The last time she'd seen it, the walls had been covered in John Cusak posters and, thanks to Mac, a few Nine Inch Nails magazine pictures.

John Cusak had always reminded her of Mac. Not in looks. obviously, but in the way he *seemed.* A fascinating mix of shy and bold. A smart kid with only so much confidence. A smart-ass guy on the edge of sensitive manhood.

Rachel pressed her head against the cheap plywood door.

"Rachel—" Her mother burst into the hallway at the other end, backlit by the yellow light from the kitchen. She looked like a character in film noir with the smoke from her cigarette trailing up her side. "Sorry. Didn't mean to disturb you."

"It's okay," she said, putting her hand to the doorknob but going no farther. "I was just going to go see if all my posters were still up."

"Nah." Eve finished wiping her hands and fisted them on her hips. "Your brother took over your room a few years after you left. We threw out a bunch of your junk, but I still have a box of it around here somewheres." She turned, headed back into the kitchen, and just like that, all the drama of standing outside the bedroom door was gone.

Now I just feel ridiculous.

She pushed open the door, flipped on the light and laughed. Her Cusak posters had been replaced by posters of helicopters, cars and *Sports Illustrated* swimsuit models.

A boy's room. And yet totally her brother's. It was so much smaller than she remembered. A glorified closet, really. One step in and she was in the center of the room. She touched the three whittling knives scattered across the desk.

"Yeah, we put your stuff in Jesse's old room. I found it, if that's what you're looking for." Eve stepped through the doorway and the room felt crowded.

Rachel eased into the desk chair to create some space. She flicked one of the knives, sending it spinning in a tight circle across the battered wood surface.

"Where's Jesse?" she asked.

The springs to the old bed squealed in protest when Eve sat. "Iraq."

Rachel hauled in a deep breath, trying to quell sudden anxiety. "Is he okay?"

"Last I heard."

Rachel watched her mother with burning eyes. "Do you hear from him a lot?"

"Once a week."

Rachel nodded and looked at her hands so her mother wouldn't see her tears. "That's good." She sighed.

"He was real mad when you left."

"So I've heard," she said, wiping her cheeks. She'd been leaking like this on and off for hours since this morning. She felt like a broken faucet. Constantly dripping for no real reason.

"He never answered none of them letters you wrote. I asked him if you kept writing him once he went away to the army and he said he told you to stop."

She nodded. How ridiculous was it that Jesse wrote his mother every week but not his sister?

Funny how betrayal works. Blame the person who got out of hell for leaving, but never blame the person that dropped you in hell to begin with.

"He's doing real good in the army. He's a ranger."

"Sounds dangerous," she murmured past the lump in her throat.

Eve sighed, her shelf of a chest heaving. "I imagine it is." She stood and the bedsprings sighed in relief. "I made some iced tea and sandwiches if you want. It's not much, but you haven't eaten all day." She turned to leave, and suddenly for Rachel forgiveness wasn't enough. It had coasted her through the past few hours with her mother, but now in her old room, missing her brother with a physical ache, she needed answers.

"Why'd you stay?" The words erupted from that dark place where the seventeen-year-old who'd been kicked out of her house still lived.

"The mortgage is paid and I—"

"Not now. Then. Why'd you stay with him?"

Eve again assaulted the bedsprings with her weight. She dug a cigarette out of the pack she had in her shirt pocket and lit it, hiding behind the smoke. "Hard to say," she finally said.

Rachel rolled her eyes. "I'm going to need more than that, Mom. He used to hit you. He beat us, your kids—"

"Okay." Eve interrupted. "But you tell me what I was supposed to do. I had no education, no money. My family was back East. He was it. All I had. He made good money and so he drank? So he got worked up? There're worse things, and I figured taking two young kids away from home to live on nothing but what I could make waitressing or worse…" The words, the images, hung in the air like grease from a fire, thick and oily and suffocating.

"You was always a smart kid. Way smarter than your dad and me. You had a million options. I had one. I did the best I could."

"Didn't you want more?"

"For me?" She blew a thick plume of gray smoke at the ceiling. She shrugged. "For you and Jess, sure. I think I did all right, making sure of that."

Rachel couldn't help her bitter laugh. "What did you do, Mom? Please. I left here because Dad kicked me out."

"Dad didn't kick you out."

"What?"

"Sure, he said the words with enough mean and drunk behind 'em to make you believe it, but getting you out of this town was my doing."

"How?"

"Well, you whisper enough things in a guy's ear when he's drinking and he starts to think it's his idea."

"But why?"

Eve dug into her pocket and pulled out two photos. She blew off a flake of ash from the top one and handed them over to Rachel, who accepted them with shaking hands.

"I saw the way the wind was blowing with that Edwards boy."

"Mac? What did he have to do with this?" She glanced at the photos. People smiling, and that didn't make sense now so she turned them over. Ignored them to concentrate on the hollow pit forming in her stomach.

"You was so smart and I wasn't gonna let you throw that away on some kid who was never gonna leave New Springs. You needed to go to college. Make money. Do whatever people do when they got money."

Rachel stood on trembling legs. "You threw me out of my home. Ruined my relationships with my brother and with Mac because you wanted me to make money?"

"I wanted you to have choices."

"Don't you think I could have done that on my own?"

Eve stood up, too, an immovable mountain convinced that she was right. "Nope. You would have stayed. You would have wanted to be with Mac."

"That would have been my choice." And it would have been. She would have stayed; she knew it like she knew her own name. A life unfurled in her imagination. She and Mac up on that mountain with children of their own. Bad jokes and family vacations and sunsets on the porch.

Rachel bit her lip and closed her eyes, but the images lingered in her mind's eye. There was no escaping what might have been.

"Well." Eve shrugged and walked out the door. "For you, at that time of your life, it would have been the wrong one."

Rachel couldn't follow her mother. She didn't want to talk about these things anymore. The past. The future. What might have been. What could be if only she and Mac could make it work. She needed to be numb. Mindless. And there was one place in this town guaranteed to bring her some peace.

She walked out of the room, down the hallway into the family room that had not changed an iota since she was twelve. She grabbed her keys and her purse, dropping the photos in her hand into the outside pocket, and headed out the door.

"Rachel? You gonna come back?"

"I'm not sure," she yelled over her shoulder.

RACHEL PARKED HER CAR behind Ace Hardware on the outskirts of town and grabbed the emergency lantern she kept in her trunk. She didn't turn it on yet, not until she was completely out of sight. She jumped the same rickety metal fence that Mr. Shoemaker had put up when she and Mac were sophomores. Her high-heeled sandals slipped on the loose gravel but she barely slowed.

She was going to relax, damn it. Get some peace even if she had to sprain her ankle to get it.

The road crested and seemed to end at a thicket of trees, but she found the trail. She flipped on the halogen light and ducked under the low branches, trying to escape the wild rosebushes that grabbed at her clothes. The trail splintered off, always to the left, but she kept walking. The trail got more overgrown, shadows, spooky and wild, danced around her. She pressed on, whacking down the overgrown weeds. Most kids didn't have the patience to walk as far as she and Mac had. And those kids settled for mediocre views and smaller overhangs. But finally after climbing over a fallen branch she took the trail to the left. It dipped and she slid on the dirt and crushed leaves, barely catching herself on a rosebush.

"Ouch," she breathed, sucking the blood from her palm. A few more steps and she stumbled out onto a granite slab overlooking the quarry.

Silence. Nothing but the wind rushing through the giant rocky hole in the ground. She sat against one of the sloping boulders and set the lantern and her purse beside her. She saw the white edges of the photos peeking out of her purse pocket and again chose to ignore them.

She didn't want to look at pictures. She didn't want to remember. She didn't want to regret what a lonely and sad life she'd had thanks to her mother.

She sighed and pulled her hair away from her face until the roots stung.

Be honest with yourself, Rachel. For once in your life.

She'd been the one to push people away, to convince herself that she was happier without family. Without love. Without Mac.

"What an idiot," she muttered, and slid down the boulder until she was sitting on the ground. She winced and brushed some of the stones from under her butt.

"I can't believe we had sex out here." She eyed the rocky ground. She hadn't noticed that night, as caught up in the moment as she had been. Which was hilarious, considering she'd later put off sex with far lesser men for reasons as stupid as the air-conditioning blowing too hard or the sheets being scratchy.

But she'd never noticed the rocks digging into her shoulders or the bugs biting her butt that night with Mac.

"Who had sex out here?"

Rachel screamed and whirled toward the familiar voice that came from her right, the opposite direction from which she'd come.

"Amanda?"

The slight girl stepped clear of the trees and bushes and into the white light of the lantern.

"Hi, Rachel." She lifted her hand in a limp wave.

"What are you doing?" A stupid question, but it was at least ten o'clock, at a rock quarry, and the girl didn't even have a flashlight. Mac would never allow this to happen.

Amanda shrugged and ripped all the leaves from a twig by her face. "I meet Christie out here sometimes."

"Does your dad know where you are?"

"No," Amanda scoffed, and stepped farther onto the granite shelf, through the light to the dark blue-and-gray shadows beyond.

"Did you just get here?"

She shook her head. "A few hours." She picked up a stone and tossed it into the void at her feet. They were at least a hundred feet up, and Amanda kept swaying toward the precipice. All of Rachel's nerve endings flared to life and she could smell trouble on the wind. "Where's Christie?"

"She went home. She said she's never going to speak to me again." Amanda's bravado cracked and Rachel could hear the tears in her voice. "What's the point of doing the right thing if it only gets you screwed?"

Rachel smiled reluctantly. "I think that's what I came out here to figure out."

Amanda turned and half her face was illuminated, ghostly and white like the granite surrounding them. "Why'd you leave today? I came home from school and you were gone."

"I couldn't stay at your house forever."

"I wish I could stay away forever," the little girl muttered. "I wish I never had to go back." She lifted her arms like a bird about to take flight and Rachel leaped up from the ground to grab her.

"Amanda! What's wrong?" She turned the girl in her arms and sucked in a breath. No tears marred her face, but her eyes were filled with painful, angry sorrow. "What's happened?"

"How do I keep doing this?" she asked.

Rachel could feel the girl's tension. She was pulled taut and trembling, ready to break. It was worse than last night. The tension that had been so unbearable a few short hours ago seemed easy compared to whatever was hurting Amanda now.

"Keep doing what?" Rachel stared into her blue eyes, willing the girl to bend before she broke. *God, I thought this was over.*

Amanda shook her head, the trembling in her arms building until she was shaking. "I thought everything was better, but I came back and you were gone!" Her voice rose to a shout. The fury in her eyes erupted. "Why did you have to leave?"

"Amanda, I can't stay at your house forever. I had to leave."

"He made you leave, didn't he?" she cried, her face red, her eyes dry. Rachel was terrified to let go of her. This was a girl bent on damage, bent on pain. "He told you to get out!"

Rachel was speechless. She opened her mouth to say something, but only a shuddering breath escaped.

"It's because of her! I hate her!" Amanda wrenched herself away from Rachel. Rachel grabbed for her but Amanda lurched backward. Stones clattered over the cliff behind her.

"Amanda." Rachel barely breathed, her eyes glued to those terrifying few inches between Amanda's tennis shoe and oblivion. "Please come away from the edge and we'll talk about it."

"I thought everything was going to be better. You spent the night. Dad seemed so happy. That night when we got the tamales, he was laughing."

Rachel caught about every third word. She focused on Amanda's feet as she bounced on her toes far too close to the edge.

"He was happy because you were happy, Amanda. He just wants you to feel better."

"Then why'd he ask you to leave this morning?"

Oh, God. "Please step away from the edge, Amanda, and we'll go back and talk to him."

"I already talked to him. He said he loved her."

"Loved who?"

"My mom."

"Well, isn't that good? I would think having your parents love—"

"She never loved him!" Amanda screamed. "She was leaving him. She was leaving us." Her knees buckled and Rachel leaped out to grab Amanda, but she jerked away.

If I can just get between her and the edge...

"What are you talking about, sweetheart? The car accident?"

Amanda squeezed her eyes shut. "It's a secret!" she cried.

"No more secrets." Rachel urged the words through a clenched jaw. "No more."

Silence. A bird squawked. Leaves lifted and ruffled in the breeze.

"What—"

"She was leaving Dad," Amanda confessed and the dam broke. Rachel got in between her and the cliff and spun her away from the danger. Amanda's words rushed out and pooled around them, almost faster than Rachel could process. "She was going to take me with her and leave Dad. I didn't want to go. She was so mean to Dad and I hated her boyfriend. I hated him so I—"

The words shook her. Margaret was cheating? *Mac. Oh, Mac I am so sorry....*

"It's okay, Amanda. It's okay. Whatever you said it's okay. You're safe. Your dad is safe."

"I grabbed her arm," she whispered. "I grabbed her arm and she jerked the wheel and that's when we crashed."

"You weren't in the back seat?"

Amanda shook her head. "I was wearing my seat belt but Mom wasn't."

Rachel gasped, horrified by what Amanda must have seen.

"I killed her."

"No!" Rachel pulled Amanda closer. "It was an accident."

"I didn't want to go with her. I hated her. I wanted to stay with my dad." She wept into Rachel's neck. Her thin, little-girl arms gripping her waist.

"Of course you did, of course." She rocked Amanda until she stopped shaking.

"He keeps wanting to talk about the accident, but how can I tell him when he says he loved Mom?" Amanda asked. "I don't want him to be hurt anymore, I just want him to be happy."

"Nothing will make your father happier than if you tell him what happened. It won't be easy, but it will make things better."

"You make him happy," Amanda sighed.

Her heart shuddered, lurched. *God, I hope so. I really hope so.* "I'm glad you think so. He makes me happy, too." *Happier than I've been since I left him.*

After a long moment Amanda pulled away. Her eyes were still dry but far less wild.

"I have to tell my dad."

"I think it's a good idea. Do you want a ride?"

Amanda nodded and they turned toward the trail.

"He's going to freak out, isn't he?"

"Does he know where you are?"

"No."

Rachel checked her watch. "Yep. I'd say he's freaking out."

"Maybe if he knows the truth about Mom, he'll… You guys can…"

Rachel smiled. Even Amanda was rooting for them. "There's a lot more between us than your mother."

"I'm sorry he asked you to leave," Amanda said. "I want you to stay."

"Thanks," Rachel murmured. Thirteen years too late, she wanted to stay, too.

CHAPTER SEVENTEEN

EVERY LIGHT IN THE HOUSE blazed against the night sky. Rachel pulled to a stop and put the car in Park.

"He's going to be so mad at me." Amanda sighed.

As if to verify her fear the front door flew open and Mac stood in the bright rectangle of yellow light, all but breathing fire. Rachel shared a look with Amanda.

That's a freak-out.

They climbed out of the car and Rachel put her arm around Amanda's shoulder in a show of support.

"Where the hell have you been!" Mac yelled.

"Dad—"

"Mac—"

"I have been losing my mind for two hours since you took off! I've got Billy and everyone down at the station going nuts looking for you." He took long, angry steps across the gravel parking area toward them. His hair stood on end and his eyes were wide with panic and worry. "You said you were doing homework in your room!"

"Dad—"

"Mac—"

"You are grounded for the rest of your life, young lady. Do you understand me? You will—"

"Mac!" Rachel yelled to cut through Mac's hysteria. "Calm down for a few minutes."

Mac seemed held in suspended animation and she knew that he was pulling back his temper, reasserting his control and all of his better sense. His red face faded to a more human color and the veins stopped bulging in his head.

There you go, she thought with a sad smile. *There's the man I love.*

"What's going on?" He bit the words out.

"Your daughter wants to talk to you." Rachel patted Amanda's shoulder and stepped away, but Amanda grabbed Rachel's hand.

"Don't go," she said.

Rachel gave her a don't-try-that-again look, but Amanda only squeezed harder.

"Will someone please tell me what's going on so I can stop having a heart attack!" cried Mac.

"Okay." Rachel sighed. "You guys talk and I'll wait for you inside." Rachel smiled at Mac. "Everything's okay," she told him as she walked past. She reached out to stroke his arm, more for herself than anything, but stopped herself, unsure how that would be perceived. It hurt to stand so near and not touch him.

In the house, Rachel turned off what lights she

could find and then pretended not to watch Mac and Amanda where they sat on the picnic table.

They were hugging a lot. Mac wiped his eyes and once she thought it looked as if Amanda laughed at something Mac said.

Good. Rachel nodded and turned from the window before she started crying. Good for them.

She needed to work out a plan. She couldn't go clear out her office until Monday, so she could stay in New Springs. Argue with her mother some more, maybe go through those— The pictures.

Rachel grabbed her purse from the island where she'd dropped it and pulled out the two photos. She took a long, steadying breath, unsure of what ghosts would greet her. She flipped them over. The first was a faded, watery Kodachrome of the whole Filmore family in one of the few happier days. Rachel was a seven-year-old girl sitting cross-legged at her father's feet with a grin—missing several teeth—stretching from ear to ear. Her father, his beer belly in its introductory stages, sat in a lawn chair with Jesse, a newborn wrapped in blankets, in his arms. Dad was leaning back, though, and Eve, standing behind him, her hair as dark as night, was leaning forward and their lips met over Jesse's head.

It was a perfect photo of a family Rachel didn't know. A good time, long forgotten, caught forever. Rachel rubbed her thumb over that square of paper that held her parents' kiss.

She would stay the weekend, repair what damage from years of neglect she could. Monday she'd go talk to Olivia and clear out her office.

And then…Rachel sighed and looked up at the ceiling as if the answers were carved into the beams. But they weren't and none immediately came to mind. She was a social worker, after all, in high demand anywhere. But maybe she'd seek out a job that didn't require so much detachment to be effective. She'd find something she could throw her heart as well as her mind into.

Olivia—since she was no longer her boss, but hopefully still her friend—would have plenty of ideas.

She flipped over the second picture and her breath caught on a laugh that quickly turned to a sob. She pressed her fingers to her lips and let the tears she'd been trying to stem all day fall.

They'd gone to the prom together their senior year. It might have been the worst idea they'd ever had, but they'd done it. Mac had gotten a tux from the money he made with the Park District and Rachel had bought a cheap red dress from Sears and then tore off all the ruffles until she could stand to wear it.

The photo had been taken on her parents' front porch and she and Mac had been so awkward, so pained by the stupid traditions of corsages and cummerbunds. They'd stood on that step like strangers rather than best friends, until Mac took the white carnation wrist corsage out of the plastic container and stretched the elastic over his head so the flowers dangled down on his face. She'd taken his boutonniere and pinned it to her dress, and then they laughed so hard the elastic on the corsage broke, snapped him in the eye and showered them with corsage petals.

That was the photo. Mac stood with his hand pressed to his eye, covered in flowers, with his mouth stretched wide open with laughter and surprise. She was bent over, holding on to his tux jacket as if she'd never let go.

I should have never let go.

She would stay in New Springs for as long as she could. For as long as it took. She would put herself in Mac's way, show him that she was ready for him. Ready to stay. Be his. Be a family.

She hoped with every fiber of her heart that whatever nebulous mysterious future was out there for her, it included Mac and Amanda. She would fight for it—tooth and nail. And she figured she had a pretty good ally in Amanda.

The front door creaked open and Mac and Amanda stepped down the stairs into the kitchen looking like weary travelers.

"Hi," she said quietly in the stillness of the empty house.

Mac smiled with half his mouth. "No one is ever keeping another secret as long as they live. Got it?" He turned a sharp eye on his daughter, who nodded.

"Got it."

Mac pulled his daughter to his side and kissed her head. He stood there for a long time, eyes closed, lips pressed to Amanda's blond hair.

"You hungry?" he asked.

"Starved."

Mac nodded and turned to the stove. Rachel saw the tears slipping slowly down the sides of his face. He bit his lip, and Rachel, her heart bleeding for him, watched him struggle for control. "Mac Edwards's grilled-cheese-and-salsa sandwiches coming right up," he finally said, the cheer in his voice forced but so welcome.

"Rach, why are you crying?" Amanda asked. Mac turned and Amanda tilted her head, and the scrutiny made Rachel hot and awkward.

"I remember your dad's sandwiches and they're enough to make anyone cry," she joked. She grabbed her purse, slipped the photo of her family inside of it, but slid the one of her and Mac across his kitchen island toward him. She darted a glance at him, but it was too painful. He was too beautiful and loved and cherished and he was currently out of her reach. Tomorrow she'd start her campaign for Mac's heart, but tonight, she couldn't stand to be treated as a friend when she so badly wanted to be his love. This was a time for Amanda and Mac, anyway. Rachel wasn't invited. Not yet.

"I'm so proud of you, Amanda." Rachel cupped

Amanda's petite face in her hands and smiled into her lovely blue eyes. "Meeting you has really inspired me."

"It has?" she asked, clearly flattered and confused.

Rachel nodded, choking on tears and wishes. "Let's make a promise, okay?"

"Okay."

"Let's fight for what we want from now on. Let's not be scared and let's not feel responsible for everything. Let's just be responsible to ourselves and let's go after our happiness. We're in charge of it, from now on."

Amanda's eyes flooded with tears. "Sounds good."

Rachel pulled the girl into her arms and said a quick prayer and thank-you that the worlds collided enough to bring Amanda into her life when she needed her most. "I love you," Rachel murmured into her blond hair. "I really do."

She set Amanda aside, gave her one more smile and then dared a look at Mac, who stood frozen, frying pan in one hand and the photo of them in the other. He looked as if he'd just witnessed a bombing.

"Where are you going?" he asked, his voice too loud for the quiet room.

She smiled, tasted tears on her lips and just kept crying. "My mom's. I've got some loose ends to tie up."

"When will…? What…?"

"You'll see me," she said. "I'm fighting for what I want, Mac." She winked at Amanda and started across the suddenly endless stretch of wood floor toward the door.

Where's the exit music when you need some, she wondered, all too aware of four eyes boring into her back.

Fight for what you want. I'm fighting for what I want. The words echoed through Mac's head, down his throat, into his chest, until they took up residence in his heart.

His blood beat out her name. *Rachel. Want. Rachel. Want.*

"Wait!" he cried, before he knew what he was doing.

Rachel paused and then turned, her gorgeous green eyes wet and worried.

"Everybody just wait a damn second," he yelled.

"Dad," Amanda said, looking intrigued and mortified.

"That's right," he told her. "I swear. A lot. And I am not going to pretend I don't anymore."

"It's cool," she muttered. She slid onto a stool and watched him with fascinated eyes.

God, he thought he'd been so honest with her. He thought that by trying to keep everything in her life normal that he was doing the right thing.

"I really screwed up," he told her, and her eyes went wide. "Bad. I screwed up bad."

"I think I should go," Rachel murmured, and she turned to leave. He knew that his future, his happiness, was trying to walk out his front door.

"Just wait!" he cried again. "Just…sit down for a second." She was so stiff, he knew she wanted to escape so she could cry and be vulnerable all by herself. But he wanted her vulnerable. He wanted her tears and her naked heart. He had to get a few things straight first. "Please. Sit."

Rachel collapsed on the steps, her lips set in a stubborn straight line while the tears kept falling.

"You're beautiful," he murmured, and she closed her eyes, squeezing more tears out.

"Maybe I should leave." Amanda stood and he whirled back around to face her.

"Sit," he ordered, barely in control of himself, let alone the two most uncontrollable women in his life.

She sat.

"Okay." He nodded, and realized he still had a frying pan and a photograph in his hands so he sat both down on the counter. Then his hands felt empty and useless so he picked the picture up again. It made him feel better.

"Your mother was pregnant when we got married. You know that."

Amanda nodded.

"And I do think that we grew to care a lot for each other. We were really happy for a long time. Your mother and I loved you so much. I—" He shook his head, too choked up to go on.

"Dad, it's cool, you don't have to say this stuff."

"No," he insisted. "I do. But when you were about seven…we stopped being so happy. I did everything I thought I should do. I tried to go to counseling. We went on trips." He swallowed. "But it became really obvious that she didn't really even like me much. That's when she started to leave and—" he said aloud what had always been too humiliating to even think "—see other men."

He couldn't look at Rachel. It was too hard to be this naked and weak in front of her, but he knew he had to do it. He heard her muffled crying and wished he could touch her, but he kept all his attention on Amanda, who watched him like a deer, all big eyes and wariness.

"I told you we were in love because I thought that was what you wanted to hear. What you needed to hear. I thought I was being honest, but I lied every day."

"It's okay, Dad."

He laughed. "You're a sweetheart, kid, and I love you more than air, but it's not okay. It was the wrong thing to do." He took a huge breath and turned to Rachel, who was using the hem of his favorite gray T-shirt as a tissue.

She winced and he laughed. Free and easy. It felt so good to do it. "And I think if we let Rachel leave tonight, it will be the wrong thing to do."

Suddenly all the air in the room was gone and the electricity that ran between him and Rachel and Amanda could have lit up the world. "I want to fight for what I want, too." His eyes never left Rachel's. "And I want you," he said. "I love—" He didn't finish his big declaration before Rachel had launched herself against him. He stumbled, her beloved weight in his arms and her tears scalding his face. Or maybe they were his.

Suddenly he was buffeted again. His daughter flung her arms around them and hung on, her body wedging its way between them, against their hearts.

He leaned back so he could see Rachel. He was offering her his bruised and battered heart, his hope, the best and worst of himself. "Stay," he whispered. "Stay with us."

"Forever." She nodded, her face aglow with a love he never thought he'd witness.

"Awesome!" Amanda howled. "Let's have grilled cheese!"

Rachel started laughing and he could feel it reverberate through his daughter, through his heart and all around his home.

*Experience the anticipation, the thrill of the
chase and the sheer rush of falling in love!
Turn the page for a sneak preview
of a new book from Harlequin Romance
THE REBEL PRINCE by Raye Morgan
On sale August 29th wherever books are sold*

"Oh, no!"

The reaction slipped out before Emma Valentine could stop it, for there stood the very man she most wanted to avoid seeing again.

He didn't look any happier to see her.

"Well, come on, get on board," he said gruffly. "I won't bite." One eyebrow rose. "Though I might nibble a little," he added, mostly to amuse himself.

But she wasn't paying any attention to what he was saying. She was staring at him, taking in the royal blue uniform he was wearing, with gold braid and glistening badges decorating the sleeves, epaulettes and an upright collar. Ribbons and medals covered the breast of the short, fitted jacket. A gold-encrusted sabre hung at his side. And suddenly it was clear to her who this man really was.

She gulped wordlessly. Reaching out, he took her elbow and pulled her aboard. The doors slid closed. And finally she found her tongue.

"You…you're the prince."

He nodded, barely glancing at her. "Yes. Of course."

She raised a hand and covered her mouth for a moment. "I should have known."

"Of course you should have. I don't know why you didn't." He punched the ground-floor button to get the elevator moving again, then turned to look down at her. "A relatively bright five-year-old child would have tumbled to the truth right away."

Her shock faded as her indignation at his tone asserted itself. He might be the prince, but he was still just as annoying as he had been earlier that day.

"A relatively bright five-year-old child without a bump on the head from a badly thrown water polo ball, maybe," she said defensively. She wasn't feeling woozy any longer and she wasn't about to let him bully her, no matter how royal he was. "I was unconscious half the time."

"And just clueless the other half, I guess," he said, looking bemused.

The arrogance of the man was really galling.

"I suppose you think your 'royalness' is so obvious it sort of shimmers around you for all to see?" she challenged. "Or better yet, oozes from your pores like…like sweat on a hot day?"

"Something like that," he acknowledged calmly. "Most people tumble to it pretty quickly. In fact, it's hard to hide even when I want to avoid dealing with it."

"Poor baby," she said, still resenting his manner. "I guess that works better with injured people who are half asleep." Looking at him, she felt a strange emotion she couldn't identify. It was as though she wanted to prove something to him, but she wasn't sure what. "And anyway, you know you did your best to fool me," she added.

His brows knit together as though he really didn't know what she was talking about. "I didn't do a thing."

"You told me your name was Monty."

"It is." He shrugged. "I have a lot of names. Some of them are too rude to be spoken to my face, I'm sure." He glanced at her sideways, his hand on the hilt of his sabre. "Perhaps you're contemplating one of those right now."

You bet I am.

That was what she would like to say. But it suddenly occurred to her that she was supposed to be working for this man. If she wanted to keep the job of coronation chef, maybe she'd better keep her opinions to herself. So she clamped her mouth shut, took a deep breath and looked away, trying hard to calm down.

The elevator ground to a halt and the doors slid open laboriously. She moved to step forward, hoping to make her escape, but his hand shot out again and caught her elbow.

"Wait a minute. *You're* a woman," he said, as though that thought had just presented itself to him.

"That's a rare ability for insight you have there, Your Highness," she snapped before she could stop herself. And then she winced. She was going to have to do better than that if she was going to keep this relationship on an even keel.

But he was ignoring her dig. Nodding, he stared at her with a speculative gleam in his golden eyes. "I've been looking for a woman, but you'll do."

She blanched, stiffening. "I'll do for what?"

He made a head gesture in a direction she knew was opposite of where she was going and his grip tightened on her elbow.

"Come with me," he said abruptly, making it an order.

She dug in her heels, thinking fast. She didn't much like orders. "Wait! I can't. I have to get to the kitchen."

"Not yet. I need you."

"You what?" Her breathless gasp of surprise was soft, but she knew he'd heard it.

"I need you," he said firmly. "Oh, don't look so shocked. I'm not planning to throw you into the hay and have my way with you. I need you for something a bit more mundane than that."

She felt color rushing into her cheeks and she silently begged it to stop. Here she was, formless and stodgy in her chef's whites. No makeup, no stiletto heels. Hardly the picture of the femmes fatales he was undoubtedly used to. The likelihood that he would have any carnal interest in her was remote at best. To have him think she was hysterically defending her virtue was humiliating.

"Well, what if I don't want to go with you?" she said in hopes of deflecting his attention from her blush.

"Too bad."

"What?"

Amusement sparkled in his eyes. He was certainly enjoying this. And that only made her more determined to resist him.

"I'm the prince, remember? And we're in the castle. My orders take precedence. It's that old pesky divine rights thing."

Her jaw jutted out. Despite her embarrassment, she couldn't let that pass.

"Over my free will? Never!"

Exasperation filled his face.

"Hey, call out the historians. Someone will write a book about you and your courageous principles." His eyes glittered sardonically. "But in the meantime, Emma Valentine, you're coming with me."

SAVE UP TO $30! SIGN UP TODAY!

INSIDE *Romance*

The complete guide to your favorite
Harlequin®, Silhouette® and Love Inspired® books.

✓ Newsletter ABSOLUTELY FREE! No purchase necessary.

✓ Valuable coupons for future purchases of Harlequin,
Silhouette and Love Inspired books in every issue!

✓ Special excerpts & previews in each issue. Learn about all
the hottest titles before they arrive in stores.

✓ No hassle—mailed directly to your door!

✓ Comes complete with a handy shopping checklist
so you won't miss out on any titles.

- -

SIGN ME UP TO RECEIVE INSIDE ROMANCE
ABSOLUTELY FREE
(Please print clearly)

Name

Address

City/Town   State/Province   Zip/Postal Code

(098 KKM EJL9)

Please mail this form to:
In the U.S.A.: Inside Romance, P.O. Box 9057, Buffalo, NY 14269-9057
In Canada: Inside Romance, P.O. Box 622, Fort Erie, ON L2A 5X3
OR visit http://www.eHarlequin.com/insideromance

IRNBPA06R   ® and ™ are trademarks owned and used by the trademark owner and/or its licensee.

Silhouette® Desire®

**Introducing an exciting appearance
by legendary
New York Times bestselling author**

DIANA PALMER

HEARTBREAKER

He's the ultimate bachelor…
but he may have just met
the one woman to change his ways!

Join the drama in the story of a confirmed
bachelor, an amnesiac beauty and their
unexpected passionate romance.

*"Diana Palmer is a mesmerizing storyteller
who captures the essence of what
a romance should be."—Affaire de Coeur*

**Heartbreaker *is available from Silhouette Desire*
*in September 2006.***

If you enjoyed what you just read,
then we've got an offer you can't resist!

Take 2 bestselling
love stories FREE!

Plus get a FREE surprise gift!

HARLEQUIN®

American ROMANCE®

IS PROUD TO PRESENT THREE NEW BOOKS
BY THE BESTSELLING AUTHOR OF THE
COWBOYS BY THE DOZEN MINISERIES

Tina Leonard

The Tulips Saloon

The women of Tulips, Texas—only thirty miles
from Union Junction—have a goal to increase the
population of the tiny town. Whether that means
luring handsome cowboys from far and wide, or
matchmaking among their current residents, these
women will get what they want—even if it means
growing the town one baby (or two!) at a time.

MY BABY, MY BRIDE
September 2006

THE CHRISTMAS TWINS
November 2006

HER SECRET SONS
February 2007

Available wherever Harlequin books are sold.

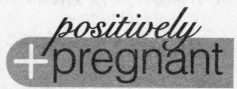

ANGELS OF THE BIG SKY
by Roz Denny Fox

(#1368)

Widow Marlee Stein returns to Montana with her young daughter, ready to help out with Cloud Chasers, the flying service owned by her brother. When Marlee takes over piloting duties, she finds herself in conflict with a client, ranger Wylie Ames. Too bad Marlee's attracted to a man she doesn't even want to like!

On sale September 2006!

THE CLOUD CHASERS—
Life is looking up.

Watch for the second story in Roz Denny Fox's two-book series THE CLOUD CHASERS, available in December 2006.

Available wherever books are sold, including most bookstores, supermarkets, discount stores and drugstores.

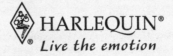

HARLEQUIN®
Live the emotion

COMING NEXT MONTH

#1368 ANGELS OF THE BIG SKY • Roz Denny Fox
The Cloud Chasers

Widow Marlee Stein returns to Montana with her young daughter, ready to help out with Cloud Chasers, the flying service owned by her twin brother, Mick Callen. Because of Mick's surgery, Marlee takes over piloting duties, including mercy flights—and immediately finds herself in conflict with one of his clients, ranger Wylie Ames. Too bad Marlee's so attracted to a man she doesn't even want to *like!*

#1369 MAN FROM MONTANA • Brenda Mott
Single Father

Kara never would've dreamed she'd be a widow so young—or that she could find room in her heart for anyone besides her husband. And then Derrick moved in across the street....

#1370 THE RETURN OF DAVID McKAY • Ann Evans
Heart of the Rockies

David McKay thought he'd seen the last of Broken Yoke when he left for Hollywood—until a pilgrimage into the mountains to scatter his grandfather's ashes forced him to return and face his first love, Adriana D'Angelo. That's when he realized the price he'd paid for his ambition. And how much a second chance at happiness would change his life...

#1371 SMALL-TOWN SECRETS • Margaret Watson
Hometown U.S.A.

It took Gabe Townsend seven years to return to Sturgeon Falls after the fateful car accident. He would never have come back if he hadn't had to. Because he still loved Kendall, and she was his best friend's wife.

#1372 MAKE-BELIEVE COWBOY • Terry McLaughlin
Bright Lights, Big Sky

A widow with a kid and a mountain of debt. A good-looking man everyone *thought* they knew. Meeting for the first time under the wide-open skies of Montana!

#1373 MR. IMPERFECT • Karina Bliss
Going Back

The last will and testament of Kezia's beloved grandmother is the only thing that could drag bad boy Christian Kelly back to the hometown that had brought him only misery....